A KILLER'S LOVE SERIES BOOK TWO

JENNIFER IVY

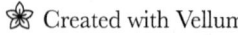

Dedication

To readers waiting and anticipating this book . . . Thank you.

TRIGGER WARNINGS

This book is a Dark Romance, and as such may contain subject matters, content, or events that you may find disturbing.

This includes but is not limited to:

Dubious Consent (Dubcon)

Blood

Gore

Kidnapping

Forced Proximity

Spanking

Anal

Breeding Kink

Mentions of restrictive food intake

Graphic descriptions of Violence, Torture, and Murder.

A KILLER'S LOVE SERIES BOOK TWO

JENNIFER IVY

CHAPTER ONE

Michael

"Come on, Duke, you know I hate it when you insist on pumping my gas."

Shaking the gas nozzle, he pulls it out of the truck. "Boy, I may be old, but I can do my own damn job." He huffs, placing the nozzle back into the pump.

A wide smile claims his face as he points a shaky finger at the flowers in the truck.

"I argued with my wife that those wouldn't sell, especially with those college kids being so close to town . . . no one's romantic anymore. Then you go and do that shit." His grin and bright eyes take away all bite from his words.

I follow his gaze to the seat of my truck, where a large bouquet of wildflowers sits next to a smaller, daintier version of the bouquet.

"What?" I grin. "I can't get my perfect niece something without getting her mother the same."

"Yeah, yeah, kid, you're real smooth." He waves me off. "My Judy will be talking about that all week."

"I have to stay the favorite uncle somehow," I tease.

The old man chuckles. "You tell that brother of yours and Charlotte that me and mine send our best. He's got himself a good woman there."

A quiet laugh slips past my lips at his choice of words. "He knows, and I will pass on your kind words," I promise, climbing into the cab of my truck. "You can call her Charlie, you know."

"Not without him glaring at me, I can't." Duke taps the top of my truck, thinking I'm about to pull off, but the sound and his words barely register. Instead, my eyes are glued to the tall, leggy brunette running toward us.

My heart jumps in my chest, and my gaze shoots behind her, looking for whoever she's running from.

My mind needs a minute to catch up as I figure out what's happening. My eyes drink her in, from the way her blue sports top clings, flowing with the curves of her body, down to the sliver of skin that appears with every few strides from where her top doesn't quite reach the top of her black leggings, the sweat on her face, the way her hair sticks to the side of her neck, the thick ponytail swinging with her strides.

Jogging. She's fucking jogging!

My heart is pounding by the time I realize it.

Fuck, can I have a heart attack at twenty-seven?

The idea of someone harming her, of her running in fear, makes my body tremble with rage.

Even though she's not in immediate danger, I can't look away. Who the fuck is she?

A bad girl, that's who.

Running with oncoming traffic at her back, what the fuck is she thinking? Someone could grab her.

A sense of déjà vu tickles at my mind.

And the irony of me teasing my brother on this very street just two years ago isn't lost on me. Daniel had a similar reaction when his now wife, Charlie, walked along this street in a similar fashion . . . suddenly, his response of spanking her doesn't seem like an overreaction.

My hands squeeze the steering wheel. The itch to punish her ass spreads through me limb from limb.

A breath stutters out of me.

"We have another Cromwell?" he teases.

I damn near fly out of my seat at the sound of Duke's voice.

So engrossed in my girl, I forgot where the fuck I was.

"Duke." I nod goodbye, ignoring his question. Starting the truck, I leave him standing beside the pump without another word.

This is what it's like to know?

Just one look at her and the thought of living without her shreds my heart.

The need to claim her, all of her, in every way possible, fills me body and soul.

Terror fills me at what would happen if she knew the real me.

No. I have to keep my distance. I will keep my distance, no matter what. With that thought, I pull off the gas station's parking lot with my eyes glued to the back of my girl as she jogs farther down the road.

I stay slow and steady, not wanting to catch up to her until she jogs onto the campus property that holds the student housing.

Stopping my truck, I watch from the road as she waves the fob over the panel next to the door before pulling it open and disappearing inside.

Worry attacks me when she's out of sight, and I know that even though I must keep my distance, I need to protect her, even if that means keeping her safe from afar.

CHAPTER TWO

Michael

"Remind me again why I'm sitting in the woods in the middle of fucking winter?"

I look over at Kaleb with a raised brow. "You're standing."

My brother huddles further into his black jacket. "I wouldn't know. I can't feel my fucking legs."

For the first time in weeks, a laugh bubbles out of me. "We've only been out here for like an hour."

"An hour too long," he complains. "Why can't you just take a page from our older brother's book and take her home with you?"

"She doesn't even know I exist, Kaleb."

"And?" He shrugs, like that fact has no bearing on the matter at all . . . and I guess it doesn't. Given our family history, it is a weak argument, but it's all I have right now. Well, all I'm willing to say out loud anyway.

The memory of how Charlie, my older brother's wife, came to be a part of our family almost two years ago fills me with warmth and want. Not because it was the last time I killed and not even because we were forced to miss our annual kill night last year but because it was the night my brother gained a partner, someone he can call his own and share his life with.

Someone who loves him for all that he is . . . his demons and his darkness.

I want that.

I want to share my life with someone who knows me, who loves me in a way that my family can't.

Someone who is just mine. But it's not meant to be, not for me.

I give Kaleb a dark look before turning my back and walking away. "I can't have that kind of life with someone. I'm not made for it."

"Why the fuck not?" I don't need to turn to see the irritation on his face. "We're all damaged, Michael. All of us. The shit we went through before the Cromwells took us in . . ." I hear his coat rustle as he shrugs. "But Daniel showed us we can be different. Have a part of our lives that's almost . . . normal." He whispers the last word, and I turn to look at my baby brother. "Can't we?" he asks quietly.

The look on his face tears at my heart.

His gray eyes, so different from Daniel's green and my blue, show his pain. Hate fills me for our shitty birth parents who made us this way. At least I had Daniel to protect and love me the best he could. Kaleb was alone before joining us at the Cromwell's.

I make my way over to him and grip the back of his neck as he hangs his head, and I find myself wishing, not for the first time, that I could pull him in for a hug.

But I just can't.

I shake at the thought of another body touching mine so fully. Instead, I squeeze tighter, hoping Kaleb won't feel the panic coursing through my body.

"You are the most hard-working man I've ever known, Kaleb. You can do anything you set your mind to. Have anything you want," I tell him.

"Not anything," he murmurs, his head still bent.

I don't correct him because who am I to argue? Sitting in the middle of the fucking woods, we're waiting for my girl to run past because although I can't talk to her, I'll die before I let anything happen to her.

Kaleb sniffs loudly, wiping his face with his coat sleeve. "Maybe you could explain. If she's as sweet as you say, she'll understand."

I chuckle softly. "Oh yeah, how's that going to go? Hey Lara, I want you to be my wife and the mother of my kids, but you can't touch me, and the only way we can fuck is from behind with your hands restrained?"

"Women like kinky shit." He grins.

"Women like your kinky shit," I correct.

Is he right?

I've fucked plenty of women. They don't seem to mind the commands and even enjoy it. But there's a big difference in one night and forever.

That's what it would be. One taste of her and I would demand forever.

I can't do that to her. I won't.

"Guess we'll both have to live through Daniel, then." Kaleb shrugs.

For now, a small voice whispers at the back of my mind.

The sound of foliage crunching under fast-moving feet reaches us a moment later.

She's here at six-thirty as always. Same time, same path, every day no matter what.

I wonder again if her running is an obsession or a compulsion.

Kaleb and I both crouch slowly, blending into our surroundings before she can see us.

Silently, we watch as Lara runs past, her movements strong and steady, like those of a confident runner.

My eyes roam over her, drinking her in as thoroughly as I can. Her long legs take her past us quickly.

She's barely out of sight before I follow. Keeping my distance, I don't bother to check if Kaleb follows. I know he is.

Like myself, his footsteps stay silent to Lara's ears, the sounds of our feet hiding under hers. Together, we match her stride.

Pride fills me at her speed. Not only is she a regular runner but she's also adept at it. Although at six foot four, I have no issue keeping up.

Thoughts of what us running together could be like tease me. Would she get mad that I slowed down for her or frustrated that I'm faster?

Never going to happen, asshole.

I follow her, watching and protecting, with my brother at my side, his words ringing in my ears.

She's wrapped up more this morning. The wind is biting and bitter. My tongue twitches with the need to reprimand her that the light jacket isn't enough. I want to dive into her life and take over every aspect, to protect and love her like only I can.

Images of Lara in my arms, round with my child and a diamond on her finger, make my cock twitch.

Arousal and sadness war within me. The knowledge of what I want and what I can have spars in my mind.

"You can't have everything you want, Michael. Sometimes in life, you just have to put up with what you have. Now stop crying and go wash your face before your brother comes back. I don't need him and your daddy fighting again."

My birth mother might have been a bitch that they should have sterilized in early adulthood, but she was right about one thing . . . we can't have everything we want.

My mood continues to sour the more we trail Lara.

I'm literally chasing my dream, and it's draining

every part of me. That is probably why my brother offered to spend his one day off this week getting up at the crack of dawn and guarding a woman who doesn't even know I exist.

I glance over at him, and Kaleb gives me an encouraging smile.

We keep pace through the woods, along the edge of town, and onto Ellis Road. The same route as always.

Same time, same route.

Hell, she's never once looked behind her since I started running with her. No self-preservation.

At least she doesn't wear her headphones every day. I roll my eyes.

My palm itches with the need to correct her reckless behavior. My girl has zero thought for her own safety. Something that will have to change. I just need to find a way to do it without her knowing it's me.

Kaleb and I continue between the thick trees, using the large trunks for cover. Not that we need to since Lara is oblivious to her surroundings.

In need of a good spanking and some firm rules.

The idea of someone else . . . of another man being the one to have that pleasure makes my stomach roil.

Distracted, I slow my feet to a walk. It doesn't take long for Kaleb to notice. He looks back at me and does a double take, worry rolling over his face when he sees mine.

"What's wrong?" he pants out.

"You mean other than you needing to step up your cardio?"

"I get enough cardio with the ladies." He winks.

I scrunch my face at that unwanted visual. "Thank you for that."

"You're welcome. Now, what's wrong?" he asks again, and I know he won't let it go until I tell him.

With a heavy sigh, I scrub at my face. "I don't know how long I can keep doing this," I tell him honestly. "She's out here running by herself. She hasn't looked behind her even once since we joined her run," I rage, flinging an arm in her direction. After licking my bottom lip, I drag it into my mouth and bite to stop anything else from spilling out.

It's not Lara I'm mad at . . . Okay, so maybe a little, but I'm the real problem. I'm the reason we can't be together. My issues are what's ruining what could have been.

This is killing me. The idea of never being with her and always watching from afar is gut-wrenching, and I'm not sure how much longer I can hold out.

"Want to stop in Duke's and grab a bite to eat?" he asks, nodding at the gas station just ahead. His mouth twitches left to right, like he wants to say something more but isn't quite sure of what to say.

Kaleb's not used to seeing me this wound up. No one is. I don't get unsettled.

Not before her.

Now, it feels like my whole world is tilting, and I'm just waiting for it to fall from beneath my feet.

But I don't say that. Instead, I nod and give my baby brother a small, grateful smile.

"I'll meet you out front with food. Can't promise I won't eat yours too, though. Judy's breakfast burgers are my current favorite meal. Duke got damn lucky marrying her. Ten years younger, and her hubby would have had some competition."

I stop sharp and throw my head back with a laugh. "That's why you joined me this morning? To come get fucking breakfast."

He gives me a wide grin.

"Little shit," I call over, shaking my head. "I'm glad you did."

"Me too."

Just as I leave, I shout back, "I'm going to tell Duke you want to steal his wife."

Kaleb gives a careless shrug as he steps out of the tree line and onto the gas station parking lot. "Go ahead. He'll tell Judy, and she'll probably give me an extra burger."

I don't bother saying anything else because who can argue with that? Instead, I pick up speed as I round the back of the building, desperate to catch up and get another glimpse of Lara.

It takes a few minutes, but when I do, all worry melts away, and I let my mind go, just breathing in the fresh, crisp winter air.

My girl and I enjoy the end of our run together, even if she doesn't know it.

CHAPTER THREE

Michael

If the building isn't on fire, I'm going to kill someone.

Yawning, I crack the passenger window. The cold air rushes in, and I fight the urge to roll it back up and crank the heat.

Freezing my balls off beats getting into a car wreck.

I blink away the tiredness as the cold air wakes my body. A glance at the dashboard tells me it's three-fifty-five a.m.

"Fuck me," I huff, rolling my neck.

The flashing lights of the responding emergency vehicles slash through the darkness as I get closer to the college campus. Red light reflects off the *Welcome to Hampstock College Student Village* sign. My family's crest stands out against the stone the sign is set in, showing anyone who looks who owns this building.

Huddles of students line the parking lot as I turn in. They look almost as pissed off as I feel at having been forced out of bed at this ungodly hour.

Almost.

My heart had practically stopped when the fire alert came through. It's not her floor, but it is her section of the building, so she'll be evacuated, too.

Nearing the students, I try not to glance over them too closely, knowing my girl should be in there somewhere.

This is her block, so she's here somewhere.

What if she's not? That little voice in the back of my head chimes, and my stomach takes a dive. Because if she's not here, then she wasn't in her own bed tonight.

I've fought with myself about how close I can be to Lara. Running with her to keep her safe? That's okay. Knowing her school schedule and occasionally following the bus she takes so I know she got there safely? That's okay. Putting a camera in her dorm to keep her safe? Not okay.

Yet.

I roll my eyes because at this point, I'm just lying to myself. It's not crossing some kind of invisible moral line that's stopped me. It's the lack of control I'll have if I know without a doubt that she's doing something with someone else.

Despite my best efforts, I do catch sight of a

handful of students, and a few of the kids look like they have yet to even go to bed.

Ideas of what they would have been doing flash through my mind along with the thought that my brother and I might have missed out. We never went to college. Mom and Dad offered to pay for it in full, but the desire just wasn't there.

Daniel hated the idea of extending his education, preferring to jump straight into a job, anything not to be in a room full of people.

At the time, my thoughts had been similar. But even if they hadn't, I have never lived more than five minutes away from Daniel, and the idea of moving to another town or state, even now, makes my stomach churn.

No, I like to live as close to my brother as I can.

If Hampstock had been open back then, I'd have a degree now, but if our upbringing taught us anything, it's that some things don't need dwelling on. Besides, things turned out okay.

I throw the car into park, and a genuine smile takes over my face as memories of the last fourteen months flood me. Charlie had been a saint to put up with both Daniel and me. Even before the birth, she was at her wits' end with our hovering.

The situation was only made worse when Daniel nearly gutted a man in a café when we had all traveled to see Charlie's family one last time before the baby came.

My insistence that I move in for the last month of

her pregnancy had almost been the final straw. I don't hold back the chuckle as I recall how her face had flushed with anger, ready to murder one of us, but after a minute, she'd scrubbed her cheeks and threw up her hands.

No point in fighting the inevitable.

Besides, the minx did have me fetching food and drink whenever the mood struck her, which was all the time at the end.

Not that I had minded. I loved it.

All of it.

The late-night cries, the dirty diapers, and the sight of Belle bonding with both her parents.

Charlie was made for motherhood. The past year, she has shown herself to be nurturing, patient, and calm, with a huge maternal instinct, which is everything I could have hoped for in the mother of my brother's children.

My heart fills at the thought of Daniel and the family he's made. The knowledge that I can never have that makes me all the more grateful that he's willing to share this part of their life with me.

After six months, it had been time to go home and leave the small family to settle into their own routine.

With the occasional drop-in, obviously.

The grin on my face doesn't leave but widens when Daniel's truck roars to a stop next to mine.

It seems I'm not the only one annoyed by the early morning callout.

Climbing out, I laugh when he slams his door so hard his truck rocks.

"Fucking students," he grunts.

"How are my girls?" I ask.

My brother tries not to react to my words. Only the fogged breath that shoots out of him shows his annoyance.

"My girls," he emphasizes, "are perfect."

I swallow the lump that lodges in my throat. Seeing Daniel smiling so easily is something I will never get over. Ever.

I make a mental note to drop off a strawberry milkshake and fries later this afternoon. Charlie liked to dip her fries in the shake while breastfeeding Belle, a craving that never left once she stopped . . . It's the least I can do.

I startle when Kaleb's car joins ours. His coupe stands out between our large trucks.

"Urgh, there had better be a fire this time. I swear to God, if one of these little fuckers set off the fire alarm cooking again, I'm going to snap a neck or two," he grumbles, walking toward us.

Daniel grunts his agreement.

I stay silent because he's right. Three callouts in two weeks for some drunk kid setting off the fire alarm cooking isn't funny, and despite our father's insistence, I'm beginning to think it's not worth the money the college pays us for the little shits to live here either.

Although that could be the two hours of sleep I've had talking.

I roll my neck again as the three of us walk toward the front of the blaring building.

Fuck me, it's loud.

My mood continues to sour the closer we get.

We're a few steps away from the curb when Daniel suddenly stops.

"What?" I ask.

Silently, he lifts his chin toward the crowd of students.

Confused, I glance over to them to see his issue, worried it's Lara.

All I see is just a bunch of drunk or tired college kids. No one stands out.

Where is she?

I must have missed something when looking for my girl because Kaleb steps toward them, anger consuming his face.

"Leave her," Daniel orders.

Who? Lara?

I look again but can't see her. A few boys in the crowd who had been scuffling get even rougher, and I catch myself doing another once-over through the crowd.

That's when I see her.

Sandwiched between two rowdy kids, my girl glares as the one behind her bumps into her, not even looking down, as if she's not there.

Fucking prick! What the fuck does he think he's doing?

My worried gaze sweeps over her. Wrapped in her fluffy blue robe with her thick brown hair piled messily on the top of her head, she's the most beautiful woman I've ever seen.

Fucking perfect. Too good for me.

My hand touches my chest, rubbing at it as if to soothe the pain of the past away. With a scowl, I drop my hand.

The past belongs in the past. I'm safe now, and the pretty girl across the parking lot doesn't belong with me.

She deserves better.

My chest tightens at the thought, and I force myself to turn away. She's okay, and I definitely can't go over there and stab someone for pushing her, right?

Daniel looks down at his watch, huffing, but he's not the only one on edge, and I'm out of patience.

I give him a look that says calm the fuck down. We both know we can't leave until the fire department clears the halls and the students are free to go back in.

As owners and the closest emergency contacts, all three of us are stuck here until we know it's safe and no one is hurt.

Kaleb is just as twitchy on my other side. One of those nights for all of us, I guess. Leaning to the left, he peers around me for the fourth time in as many seconds.

I'm unsure what he's looking at, so my mind returns to the pretty brunette behind me. *Does she need me to intervene? Is she still being pushed around?* I roll my neck again but force myself to stay where I am.

My muscles feel like they're vibrating. I need to hit someone. We're not missing out on kill night again this year. We all fucking need it. This week cannot pass quickly enough.

My body shivers in anticipation.

Another scuffle behind me has me picturing two perfect targets. Sunday is going to be the best night in years.

"Hey!" a female voice calls out, and even from this distance, I just know it's my girl.

I spin, marching toward the students before I can even register what I'm doing. Kaleb's stride matches my own, his face just as tense and thunderous as mine, and confusion fills me once more.

My mood darkens further. If he thinks my girl is his, he can fuck right off. Brother or not, no one is taking her home except me.

No, I'm not . . . Fuck!

I scrub a hand over my face, but it does nothing to stop the warring inside my head, nor does it wipe away the thunderous look on my face as we near the rowdy group. She's caught between the two hyper pricks, and just seeing that scared look on her face as she's jostled again, I know I'm about to break both of the rules I give my brothers—no killing outside of Halloween and no witnesses.

My fingers twitch. The need to wrap them around one of their necks surges through me. It doesn't matter which; either will do. Kaleb can stab the other. He won't mind. He likes that.

But we don't make it that far. I stop short when Kaleb cuts in front of me, his hand reaching out to grab the back of a woman's dress, but she's quicker than he is.

Sidestepping, she squats down and squeezes farther into the crowd.

What is he doing? Who the fuck is that?

I'm about to leave him and, apparently, his girl to it, but he shoves the guy blocking his way. And while I wouldn't normally question his ability, this guy is big. No way am I about to leave my little brother to fend for himself when a college frat boy and his friends are about to descend.

Stepping up behind Kaleb, I eye the two fuckers who decided to join the fray with a smirk on my face.

This is exactly what we need.

The two boys in front of me turn pale, backing up quickly.

I don't even need to turn to know why. *Fucking Daniel.*

My body tenses even more, knowing that no one will start a fight with my older brother around. Kaleb and I are built, but Daniel is a fucking wall.

A large hand squeezes my shoulder, but again, I don't look. Only one person can touch me without my body panicking. "Your rules, brother." I can hear the smile in Daniel's voice.

Asshole. Since when did he cut the fun short? I

preferred it when he didn't talk . . . no, I didn't. I hated it. I love Charlie for being able to bring that part of him back to me.

I nod once because as much as I'd love to kill someone right now, I know better. And so does Kaleb.

Our little brother stands a few feet in front of us, toe-to-toe with who looks to be the college linebacker.

"Little girl, you can either come out here now, or I can break your boyfriend's face and then drag you out. The choice is yours."

Like everyone else out here, Daniel and I stand watching, waiting to see how this plays out.

A hand peeks out from between the crowd of bodies, catching on the footballer's jersey as she tries to pull herself through the people blocking her. When her hand slides over the guy's chest, trying to get a better grip, Kaleb growls.

Reaching out, he wraps his hand around hers and yanks her out of the group.

Samantha stands before us. Her hair mussed as she tries to pull the hem of her short dress farther down her thighs with her free hand.

"Hi, guys." My sister smiles sheepishly. "I was just out with friends. I should get back," she says, pointing her thumb over her shoulder, but Kaleb's not letting go.

I think the fuck not!

"What are you, like, her dad?" the dumbass behind her asks.

Kaleb shakes his head. "Do I look old enough to be her fucking dad?"

A few of the kids around us laugh, and the guy behind Sam squirms, his cheeks turning red.

Stepping back, Daniel nods to the parking lot. "Car, I'll see if we can hurry this along."

We only get a few steps when Sam resists. "Wait, wait. My shoes."

Our gazes snap to her feet. "Where the fuck are your shoes?"

Giving a stressed smile, she points at the building.

Kaleb takes a deep breath and then another. It doesn't work. "Why were you not wearing shoes?" he snaps.

"Because I was inside his apartment . . . obviously." She huffs back, pulling her hand free.

"Dude, she doesn't want to go with you," Jersey shirt shouts, apparently having recovered from his earlier embarrassment. Or maybe he's feeling bold now that a few rowdier kids have joined him from farther down the line. My eyes flick back to where they had been before, but I look away quickly.

Knock it the fuck off. She's surrounded by people. Lara's okay.

My already shitty mood takes a deeper dive, and I'm not the only one.

Daniel steps closer to our brother and sister, his face a blank mask hiding his annoyance. These are supposed to be quick callouts to confirm that everything and everyone are okay, but each time seems to be taking longer and longer.

"Car, now." Daniel's sharp tone is all it takes to get both Sam and Kaleb moving again.

But Samantha just can't help herself. "What're you in such a rush for? It's the middle of the night. What could you have been doing that was so important?"

"My wife." Daniel glares.

My mouth twitches at Kaleb's snort, but the disgusted look on Sam's face makes me smile. Quietly, I swallow my laugh.

We make it a few more steps. "Cold, cold," Sam hisses, hopping.

Kaleb tuts, steadying her by the elbow. "That wouldn't happen if you had shoes on, girl." But despite his tone, he slides his arm around her back, trying to lift her, only to have his hand slapped away.

"Yeah, well, I wasn't planning on coming back outside just yet."

My brother's face darkens. "No shit, we all know exactly where you planned on coming."

"Fuck off."

He should have just thrown her over his shoulder.

"Enough," Daniel snaps, scrubbing his forehead. "Kaleb, put her in the car."

With that encouragement, my baby brother flashes us a triumphant grin, then throws Sam over his shoulder with a small grunt and strides toward his parked car.

"Asshole, you did not just grunt picking me up!"

Now I do laugh. Standing near the crowd, I'm entertained as I watch Kaleb grapple to keep a squirming Sam on his shoulder. A sound spank to the ass suddenly stops her movement.

The two blonds have everyone's attention.

I stay where I am as Kaleb opens his car door. He dumps a seething Sam on to the back seat, shoves her legs in, and slams the car door.

His whole body is tense as he glares at her through the window. "Stay," he orders, pointing at her.

A thud echos out as Sam kicks the inside of the car door. Kaleb's gasp is lost in the noise, but his open mouth tells me he's as shocked as I am.

Before I can think too hard about the scene before me, a heavy hand shoves at my shoulder, forcing me to take a step to keep my balance.

Someone wants to die tonight.

Breathing in deep, I turn to face the little dick. I don't even try to hide my fury.

His face quickly pales, and his two friends step back.

"Come on, dude, kick his ass another time," one of his friends murmurs.

I don't take my eyes off Kaleb's jersey guy who touched me, not even to blink.

"Yeah," he agrees cockily, stepping back, but he's not smiling anymore. "Next time."

"Next time," I promise with a nod. He stumbles backward, and my eye twitches with disappointment.

The boys force their way farther into the crowd, causing everyone to push and shove at one another again.

My eyes move on their own, peeking in Lara's direction just in time to see my girl get jostled in the crowd again. What little hold I have on myself snaps.

I don't think; I just move.

My feet carry me through the crowd quickly. I'm not far when the crowd suddenly surges, and she's squeezed out.

With a loud cry, Lara falls to the ground, face twisted with pain, and I see red. Shoving at the guy closest to her as hard as I can, I force him to fall flat on his back and away from her. The others nearby rush to step away, the group spreading farther back.

Behind me, I vaguely hear the sound of running. Two heavy sets of feet hitting the asphalt remind me my brothers have my back.

Like always.

Safe in that knowledge, I do something I've never done before. I turn my back on a threat and crouch down before my girl.

I give her a soft smile. "You okay, baby?"

The ball of messy brown hair at the top of her head swings back and forth as she shakes her head. "No." She sniffles.

I zone out of the noise behind, trusting my brothers to protect us.

Us. The word makes me warm, like we're not outside in the middle of winter.

My eyes roam over her quickly, looking for an injury. "What hurts?" I demand. My heart hammers in my throat, and I swallow, trying to shove my panic down.

She's okay. No blood, no broken bones.

"My ankle," she whispers.

I nod at the top of her head. "Okay, let me feel," I tell her, reaching out to take her foot.

"No, no!" Panicked, watery brown eyes plead with me as her hands shield her ankle.

"Baby, you have to let me touch it so I can see what's wrong." I try to soothe her.

She shakes her head. "Nuh-uh." Her face is scrunched in a scowl. I'm not getting anywhere near her injured leg.

"Okay," I concede, holding up my hands.

Shifting, I rest my knee on the hard ground. The cold seeps in quickly, and my eyes drop to where her robe cushions her. It's fluffy but thinner than I thought. Not much of a barrier between the cold ground and her ass.

I stroke a finger over one of the small yellow ducks that litter the blue material.

"He's cute."

Her smile melts me.

She can't stay here.

"You have one of two options, princess. You let me look at that ankle, and we can get you sorted quickly, here and now, or we move you over to the car, and you let me look at it there."

Lara glances behind me, then she leans forward, looking at our cars.

"They're warmer." I try to entice her. I'm not sure why I encourage her. Maybe I want her away from the crowd, or maybe I just want her in my truck.

There's a scuffle behind me, and Daniel's voice growls, "That is the only warning you'll get, boy."

"Warning? I think you broke my fucking nose." Someone groans. "You're the rich brothers who own this building. I'm gonna sue. You fucking wait."

"Sue for what, dipshit? You tried to hit him first so you could get to an injured girl behind us," Kaleb taunts.

Well, that decides it.

I don't look back to see who he hit nor do I care.

My girl has my whole attention.

"What's your name, princess?" I ask her gently, wanting her to tell me so I can use it. It's not like I can admit I've been stalking her for weeks . . . and know her name and so much more already. "I'm Michael," I add with a nudge under her chin.

"Lara, but I kind of prefer princess," she answers with a watery smile. Her eyes shine, big and wide. Her cheeks are red from the cold.

"Me too." I wink with a grin. My heart pounds as she blinks innocently up at me. "Okay, princess . . ." I pause, letting the name sink in. I really do prefer it. "I'm going to carry you to the car now."

"No, no. I can walk," Lara insists.

Sliding one arm around her waist and the other

under her bent legs, I stand, lifting her. "I wasn't asking, princess." I press a kiss to the crown of her head to soften the blow, but this is how I am and something she'll get used to.

No.

I need to remind myself why this isn't for me and why she isn't for me.

Daniel did it.

Just as a kernel of hope unfurls, I feel her hand brush my stomach and become aware of the way her shoulder presses into my chest.

Panic fills me, and my heart pounds. I need to put her down, but I can't let her go, not even for a second.

Pain rips through me at our contact. I hate myself more with every step.

I take us past my truck because if she goes in, I'm not sure I'll let her back out.

Annoyed, I kick the door to Kaleb's car, nodding for Sam to open it.

Gently, I place Lara on the back seat as Sam shuffles over.

"One more person kicks my fucking car, I swear to God," Kaleb bitches.

Sam and I roll our eyes as I crouch in the open doorway.

"Okay, princess, let me see," I say, reaching for her right leg.

"No," she declines. Seeing my raised brow, Lara adds, "No . . . thank you." A cheeky grin plays on her lips.

"I won't ask again, princess. Your foot." Holding my hand out, I wait.

"Or?" she challenges.

"Or he'll give you a sore ass," Kaleb murmurs from behind me, pushing his way between me and the car door.

Sam shuffles in her seat behind Lara. "And you'd know all about that," she mumbles.

Kaleb gives our sister a dark look. "Not that kind of sore ass." Turning back to my girl, he gives a surprised look. "Well shit, if I'd have known it was you, Fawn, I would have carried you over here myself."

The fuck you would.

"Fawn?" I ask. What the fuck is he talking about? He knows Lara's name. I've talked of nothing and no one else since the day we met.

Sam glares at Kaleb from inside the car, just as annoyed as I am.

My younger brother turns to me with a grin that tells me he's about to piss me off more. "We run together most mornings."

What the fuck is he up to?

Is this what Daniel felt like when he met Charlie? I ask myself as I fight the urge to stab him in some way.

Lara frowns. "No, we don't."

With wide eyes that flick back and forth between my brother and me, Lara tentatively places her foot into my outstretched hand.

"Good girl," I praise her, but my hands tremble as

I try to ignore Kaleb's grin. "Fawn?" I ask again, my voice sharper than intended.

"She's cute and small, with big brown eyes . . . It's definitely not because of the way she runs." He winks.

Lara gasps, clutching at her chest. "I'm injured, and you're insulting me?" Her words trail off with a chuckle.

My lips curve at the way she sounds genuinely insulted.

It's cute. She's cute.

"We don't run together," she reassures me with a shake of her head. As if she's worried that I believe they do.

Kaleb tuts next to us, leaning his elbow on the roof of the car. His smile widens again. I know I'm not about to like what I hear. I just pray it doesn't tip me over the edge. "Sure, we do. We run through the wood path from the dorms, along the edge of town and down Ellis Road past Duke's gas station back to the college village."

My whole body tenses.

"Seven miles every morning. No excuses."

His words may have been directed at Lara, but his eyes were on me. He knows I don't want to pursue her. Is this his way of forcing my hand?

"Ahh," Lara shrieks, her foot twitching in my grip.

Guilt consumes me, and I relax my hold. My thumb strokes back and forth on the pale skin peeking out between her fluffy socks and the bottom of her cotton pajama pants. "Sorry, baby."

"Does she need a doctor?" Daniel asks.

"No, she's perfect." I smile up at her before glaring at my younger brother. "But Kaleb might need one," I warn.

Lara's eyes are wide, her words whispered. "I don't run with him."

He shrugs. "Like I said, you're small and cute. You shouldn't run alone, it's dangerous."

"You stalked me?" she hisses.

Now who's the dipshit.

"Protected. And not me," he corrects, nodding toward me.

My face heats, and I'm fucking blushing. *I'm going to kill him.*

"Your bodyguard let me tag along yesterday," he adds. *Can he not keep his mouth shut?*

Lara looks at me like I'm some kind of serial killer. The irony isn't lost on me. I plead with my eyes for her to understand. My stomach sinks further when her gaze drops away. Is she scared?

Fucking Kaleb.

The whole car shakes, and my hands fly to Lara's waist. The robe is soft and smooth but does nothing to hide the feel of her body underneath. She feels fragile in my large hands. I wait for the panic to settle in from touching another person, but it doesn't come.

I'm still confused about what just happened when Sam raises her leg and drives it into the back of the seat in front of her again, rocking the vehicle.

"Knock it the fuck off. I won't warn you again

tonight, Samantha," Kaleb snarls. "What is it with people kicking my fucking car!"

"Well, take me home then, if you're finished fucking flirting, that is," our sister hisses, kicking the seat again. "Or better yet, let me go back to my new friend."

"Samantha." At his tone, Sam sniffles and slouches further into her seat.

Lara sits trapped between the two at the edge of the back seat, startled and scared. Something solid settles in my stomach at the thought of her being afraid when I'm right here.

"You're safe," I reassure her. "I got you, princess. Kaleb's just having a tantrum. He loves his car."

Her big doe eyes blinking down at me is the only response she gives. Her chest heaves rapidly.

Huh, maybe Fawn is the right name for her.

I shake my head and cradle her foot again. My hand works its way up her cream pajama pants, stroking along her shaking calf.

"It's too cold out here, but when you go in, take your sneaker off and prop your foot up. You can keep the cute socks on," I tease.

I tickle at a duck on her robe, earning a reluctant smile.

"Tantrum? Me?" Kaleb rolls his eyes, ignoring everything but the insult. "It's not me protecting my car that you need to worry about now, Fawny," he teases, nudging me with his foot. "Wait until this asshole remembers that the first time he saw you,

you were running down Ellis Road alone at six a.m."

"So?" she challenges, not looking as she knocks my hand away from another duck.

"Absolutely no regard for your own safety. Nothing a good spanking won't sort out."

"Oh, so you're the funny brother." Lara laughs, but it's nervous. She's still hoping Kaleb's words are a joke. I guess she's going with denial, which works for me.

"Yep, and these two are dumb and dumber."

With a deep breath, I try to remind myself of why I can't hit my little brother . . . *Yeah, I got nothing.*

"No, he's the quiet one, and quiet doesn't mean stupid," she tells him, pointing behind me to Daniel.

"Which brother does that make me, princess?" I ask as I hear Daniel walk away toward the main building.

Hopefully, we can all get the fuck out of here.

"The hot one," she whispers and shivers as my hand settles on the back of her knee. "And a stalker."

"Right answer, and I wasn't stalking." Her shoulders relax slightly. "I was protecting." Lara freezes. The cat's out of the bag, thanks to Kaleb, so I might as well be honest. I grin, loving the blush that settles on her cheeks. "But we're still going to discuss you running alone. It stops now, Lara." Turning her gently, I tuck her legs into the car

My girl ignores my tone and chirps, "We'll see."

"Yes, princess, we will," I promise, pressing a kiss

to her forehead. "I'm going to finish up here." I nod to where Daniel and Kaleb stand talking to the fire chief. "Then we'll go home and have a chat."

Not waiting for a reply, I stand and close the door between us.

My heart hammers in my chest as I watch her shy smile turn confused. Again, I can't stop thinking about Daniel and Charlie and how far they've come as a couple. Of how much Charlie loves her husband, all of him.

Can I have that? Can we have that?

She didn't panic too much or run away when Kaleb told her I protect her in the mornings. Not that she could run on that ankle.

Fuck.

CHAPTER FOUR

Lara

The sound of the car door closing clears my head.

Shit . . . what was that?

Movement next to me reminds me that I'm not alone.

"Hi. Samantha, right?" I ask with a small, awkward smile.

"Whatever." She barely looks at me but kicks the seat again.

A large hand slaps down on the car window, startling us both. "Behave," Michael orders, pointing at Samantha. "Or it won't be Kaleb you deal with this time, Sam." His voice might be muffled, but it takes nothing away from the threat, and I swallow, anxiety fluttering in my chest.

He's not even mad at me, and I feel bad.

Has he really been following me? Or do we just run the same route? I see some runners but not many. I like running early because everyone's still in bed. That and it gets my daily exercise out of the way.

Once he's happy with her nod, Michael turns his pointed finger to me. "Stay in the car until I come fetch you."

It's not a question, but I nod anyway, happy when his scowl turns into a grin. With a solid nod of his own, Michael turns and walks toward the other two men.

His jacket pulls firm along his broad shoulders. The man's built. His features are similar to the larger man, but his hair is slightly longer and perfectly in place. Had he been out before the fire alarm?

Kaleb's blond hair stands out among the group of brunettes.

A sudden thought hits me.

"Michael's not your boyfriend, is he?"

Sam's face scrunches. "Eww, no."

Why does that make me happy? I can't even get into that thought right now.

"One of the others?" I check.

"No! They're my brothers . . . kind of. It's complicated," she snaps.

Sniffing, I wiggle my warming fingers. Michael was right. It is much warmer in here than out there.

Together, we watch as the three brothers talk to a firefighter. His face is drawn into a stern frown and is as red as his hat.

Cooking accident, again. I roll my eyes.

Sam fidgets beside me, but I stay quiet, not wanting to upset her more. Hopefully, I can return to my dorm soon and sleep the rest of the night away.

First, I got fired from my waitressing job at Lowe's because I wouldn't sleep with my boss—like a married, forty-four-year-old is on the list of things I need. Then I couldn't even sulk in peace because someone can't cook, and to top off my day, I somehow managed to sprain my ankle, only for the hottest guy I've ever met to see.

And, oh yeah, he might be my stalker.

I shiver again, but I'm no longer cold. I try to think back if I've ever seen them running in the morning, but I haven't. Michael's not the type of man you forget seeing.

"Kaleb was joking about following me, right?" My words trail off into a breathy laugh.

Sam tears her attention away from the four men, her eyes piercing me with a glare.

Shit.

I quickly swallow the saliva filling my mouth.

"Of course, he fucking was," she huffs, slumping back into her seat. "Why would he follow a plain Jane like you?" Her eyes drift back to where the brothers stand.

Plain Jane.

Her words hit their mark.

Why would he want a plain Jane like me?

The sound of my mother's voice echoes around

inside my head. *"No one wants a plain Jane, Lara. Should you be eating that? Have you done your run today? You look like you put a few inches on your waist. Get on the scale."* The nickname mocks me, and I suddenly feel twelve again.

My eyes fill with water, and my stomach roils.

Can't this day just fucking end?

Squeezing my eyes closed, I try to extinguish the past. I will myself not to cry, but the corners of my mouth tug down, and tears creep out, wetting my lashes.

My chest rises, and a sob chokes me. I try not to make a sound; it always made my mother worse.

Not that Sam would hear. She's too busy kicking the back of the front passenger seat.

The breath finally escapes through my mouth, leaving only exhaustion behind.

Can we go back in yet?

My teeth sink into my bottom lip to stop the way the corner of my mouth quivers down, but it's no good. Instead, I twist my lips left, then right.

I will not sob in this car! Pushing up, I sit straighter, ignoring the pain that pierces my ankle.

Michael is blurry as I look out, but it's not hard to see the way his face drops. Something in my chest blooms at his obvious concern, but then the car roars to life beneath me, and I realize he wasn't frowning at me.

No, the reason he and Kaleb are sprinting toward the car is the nutty woman sitting in the driver's seat, throwing the vehicle into drive!

Lost in the past, I completely missed Sam climbing into the front.

My body is thrown back into the seat a little as she peels out of the parking lot.

"Uh, Sam?"

The petite blond startles, like she forgot I was even in the car.

I really am forgettable.

Glancing in the rearview mirror, she rolls her eyes but stays silent as the car leaves the parking lot and joins the main road.

I grip the door like my life depends on it because I honestly think it does. Who the fuck taught this girl to drive, Kyle Larson?

I grapple quickly with my seat belt because I don't have a death wish, which is more than I can say for the other woman in this car.

We fly down Ellis Road at what must be twice the legal limit. My stomach roils for an entirely different reason than it did earlier, and as we pass Duke's station, the lights all melting together, I think I might get car sickness for the first time in my twenty-one-year-old life.

Vomiting all over myself and the back seat will definitely push the night over the edge and officially into the "worst night of my life" category.

The tires scream, or was that me? As we take a left so fast that the back of the car swings out, it sways this way and that as Sam tries to regain control before we finally collide with a tree.

A fucking tree!

I look at the passenger's side, where the door curves inward as if the metal is reaching out to me. Thankfully, she managed to slow down a little before we collided. Who knows what would have happened if she hadn't. The popping sound of metal hitting wood plays over and over in my head as I take a mental note of my limbs.

Head—*check*. Arms—*check*. Legs—my ankle now feels like it's on fire, but it's still attached, so *check*.

Gently, I pull at the seat belt where it digs into my shoulder, prying it away slowly. My ribs scream when I breathe in deep.

Better a bruised shoulder and sore chest than a cracked head, I remind myself.

Speaking of brain damage, a loud, obnoxious laugh bursts out of Sam. I can't see her face, but I do see the red on her fingers when she pulls them back from her forehead.

Shit.

"Oh, he's going to love that." She chuckles to herself.

Still stunned at what just happened, I stay quiet in the back seat. Sam starts the car again and continues down the private drive like nothing happened.

I think she's forgotten she's not alone again. But after that show, I'm not about to remind her.

Somehow, this last stretch of road feels longer than the entire drive. That's probably because we're only doing thirty, and there are not many things I wouldn't do right now to get out of this car.

I eye the door handle but shake it off quickly. There's no point in breaking my neck as well as my ankle.

The throbbing gets worse the more I think about it, and I breathe out a shaky breath. God, I hope Michael was right, and it's not actually broken. That will definitely set me back. Even just twisted, I know I will need to be careful for the next few days, but the thought of missing more than one morning run spikes my anxiety.

The idea of falling back into old habits causes a few more tears to fall, and I try to push out the voice telling me I'll get fat and that no one will love me.

Closing my eyes, I take deep, steady breaths, letting my mind fall empty just like Doc Jane taught me in high school. And as my thoughts retreat, I make a note to email her for a chat this week.

In and out.

In and out.

In and out.

Be in this moment, I remind myself.

The voice with harsh words that sounds remark-ably like my mother fades further and further away until I'm left with peace. My body slumps back into the seat beneath me, and my muscles feel loose from exhaustion.

With one last heavy breath, I open my eyes, only to immediately scowl.

We've stopped. And I'm alone.

All of my newfound peace quickly leaves me. I'm in the middle of nowhere, injured, just been in a car crash, and now I've been abandoned to die alone.

Panicked, I sit up quickly. It's still dark out, too dark to really see where I am.

The smell of the water says I'm near the town lake. A large wooden cabin on my right is the kind you see in romance films. I know it's cozy and warm without even going inside. There's only one large house on this side of the lake. They really are the Cromwells.

The top floors are dark, while light spills from the ground-floor windows onto the front porch.

The large wooden steps tempt me. Can I knock? Force my way inside and demand she take me home? No, definitely not that. I'm never getting in a car with her again.

Twisting in my seat, I peer out of the back window, but the light only reaches so far, and other than the start of the dirt road we came down, the only things visible are a handful of huge trees. The darkness reaches out, trying to engulf that too.

The blackness beyond the first few trees is starting to creep me out. The stillness of the night is a stark reminder that I'm out here alone. Anything could happen, and no one would know.

Decision made.

Shifting in my seat, I tug the door handle and step out of the car.

Big mistake.

My leg crumples beneath me, and pain ricochets from my ankle up my leg and back down again, where it settles.

I cry out as my weight falls forward, but I refuse to end this awful night by face-planting on the ground. Twisting, I grab the doorframe to save myself, but it just reminds me of the damage the seat belt did to my shoulder.

Pain.

That's all I feel. My ankle, my shoulder, my ribs, my pride.

Can this night just fucking end?

CHAPTER FIVE

Michael

"We're going to head back to the station and complete the paperwork," Chief Cole informs us. "The kids can go back in now, but uhhh, if you don't want to tell them just yet, I don't mind filling out the paperwork in the truck."

A smirk tugs at my lips. The man is clearly as fed up with these kids as I am.

I like his thinking.

Next to me, Kaleb claps his hands loudly. "I got this." He grins.

"Right, you little shits. It was another fake callout for a cooking accident."

Groans rise from the crowd as they quickly shuffle forward.

"Nuh-uh." Kaleb stops them by walking to the

front of the crowd and blocking them. "Which moron thought they could cook ramen with a Bunsen burner?"

Unsurprisingly, no one speaks out.

"Okay, okay." Kaleb nods. "Snitches get stitches. I can respect that."

Where is he going with this? I give both Daniel and Chief Cole a shrug when they give me a look, wondering the same thing.

Who cares? As long as it stops these callouts, my brother can have free rein.

"How about instead of stitches, the snitch gets to go back inside and snore their little head off?" He tries to bargain, pointing at the front of the building where a few firefighters stand, blocking the door.

Again, silence is the only answer he gets.

"Like the rest of my family, I don't like to ask twice. Who set off the fire alarm by cooking on a tiny fucking flame?" Kaleb demands, his patience waning. His tone questions how someone even thought to cook that way.

Fair because what moron uses their chemistry set to cook a snack in the early hours of the morning? A drunk moron. Who else would be dumb enough to put a plastic ramen cup over a naked flame?

We're lucky melted plastic and a small carpet burn are the only damage done or so Chief Cole says.

Did they think they were having a fucking cookout?

Kaleb's voice brings me out of my thoughts.

"Okay, no snitches. You're all in this together, then. Cromwell has one fire truck, so being here could have cost innocent lives. These hardworking men who could have been needed at a real emergency will chill in their big truck while you losers run the length of this parking lot ten times each. And then the fire-fighters will line up, and you can all apologize to them individually."

The crowd of college kids roars to life with loud complaints, bitching about how unfair life is.

If they only knew.

"You can't do that. I'll call my father," one kid threatens, his voice rising above the rest.

"Good." Kaleb nods. "He can come run with you. He deserves it for not making sure you were smarter. What's your name, kid?"

"Alex," he answers, losing some of his bravado.

Kaleb points. "Due to Alex having a big mouth, it will now be fifteen laps. You can thank Alex as you run past him."

No one moves.

"You're not getting inside until you run and apologize. Actions have consequences."

Kaleb's spread legs and folded arms just add to his "I'm not moving on this" attitude.

"Is he serious?" Cole asks.

"Oh yeah." I chuckle.

Chief Cole pauses before nodding. "Well, okay then. Gents, you heard the man, we have paperwork. Nixon and Pepper, you two stay by that door just in case one of these students decides they're too good for the consequences of their actions."

More and more objections get thrown out, but it doesn't take long for them to realize Kaleb means it.

The first person steps forward, a girl. Short, with a cute round face.

"What are you doing?" one of the boys hiss.

"I'm not staying out here all night. I'm cold and tired and wanna go to bed."

"What's your name?" Daniel asks her.

"Caroline," she answers nervously, her eyes flicking among Daniel, Kaleb, and us.

"Caroline, you get to do five."

Her face lights up with a bright smile. Running over to us, she raises her hand to my brother. My six-foot-seven, permanent scowl on his face brother.

Kaleb and I laugh as Daniel raises his hand to chest height for himself and watches stone-faced as she hops up to high-five him.

Even Chief Cole chuckles. "Let's hope this instills some common sense, shall we?" He's quick to join his men when, one by one, the kids start to run the length of the parking lot.

"Do you need me?" Daniel's voice rumbles next to me.

Turning to look at him, I see him check his watch for the hundredth time tonight.

"Always," I tell him gently.

The image of Lara, visibly upset in the back of Kaleb's car, makes me pause, but she's with Sam. My sister might be mad, but she's not entirely irresponsible. She'll take care of Lara until I get there. "But we can handle tonight. Send my girls my love."

Daniel stares at me, not saying a word. Those who don't know better would think he would love to punch me in the face, but I do know better.

I wait.

"Kaleb's her favorite uncle."

I gasp, loud and dramatically, clutching at my chest. "You did not just say that!"

My big brother just smirks and heads to his truck.

"Take it back! You take it back," I shout after him.

I see his shoulders shake, and warmth fills me, pushing out the pain of the past a little bit more. I will forever be in debt to Charlie, even if she doesn't know it.

CHAPTER SIX

Michael

True to his word, Kaleb keeps us outside until every one of them runs their fifteen lengths.

As the last few stragglers walk back toward us, I regret not joining them. I'm freezing my balls off out here.

Between the cold and worrying about Lara, I'm more than ready to get out of here.

"That the last one?" I ask Kaleb as he approaches.

"Yeah, Chief and his boys are headed back to base now. Told them I'd drop off some donuts on my way to work in the morning as a thank-you for being patient tonight."

"Thanks. It's always good to be in their good

graces although they seemed to enjoy the show." I chuckle.

"No problem, they seemed to appreciate the offer. I think." He frowns. "They were too busy laughing at a police joke Nixon told as soon as I mentioned donuts."

My brother gives me a little smirk, and together, we head toward my truck.

Kaleb groans next to me. "She took my fucking baby."

I smother my laugh, but nothing can stop the smile that spreads across my face.

Sam has no idea how much he loves that car . . . or maybe she does. I push those thoughts away quickly. I have refused to think about their relationship for a while, so a little longer won't hurt. Besides, I don't have time for that brand of crazy right now.

Instead, I ask, "Do you want me to drop you off at home?"

Kaleb shakes his head. "I need my car for work at seven . . ." He pauses to glance down at his watch. "Which is in an hour and a half. Jesus Christ," he cusses. "You heading to go get your girl?"

Grabbing the door handle, I glare at him through the truck where he stands on the other side. "I don't have a girl. And what the fuck was earlier about?"

"What was what about?" he asks, playing dumb.

Climbing behind the wheel, I huff, "Telling Lara I stalk her."

Kaleb just shrugs. Shrugs!

"Dude, relax. She thought I was joking. Besides, look on the bright side. She didn't freak out, and now you know she thinks you're hot."

"No, she thinks I'm a weirdo. You didn't see her face when Sam drove off. Poor girl looked like she wanted to cry," I mutter. Maybe that's the real reason I was willing to stay and not rush after the girls. Lack of sleep is catching up, and defeat is creeping in.

"Lara's interested. You just have to put yourself out there," Kaleb coaxes me, his voice losing his signature playful tone.

Fuck.

I was hoping I could put this conversation off a little longer . . . forever, preferably. Some things you just can't take back once they're out there.

We fall into silence. Kaleb is lost in his thoughts while I try to think of the best way to broach the ever-looming subject without him burning the bridge I'm offering.

While our older brother would burn the bridge to protect himself, Kaleb is the kind of man who lights it on fire just to watch it burn.

Once on Ellis Road, I take a deep breath.

"Daniel means the world to me. He literally saved my life." I glance at Kaleb and find him frowning at me.

"I know." He nods.

"I wouldn't be here if it weren't for him." Emotion fills me, and I blow out a harsh breath.

Kaleb stays quiet for a moment before whispering, "I know."

"The shit that went on in that house before the Cromwells took us in . . ." I pause with a shake of my head because, even now, it's not something I can easily talk about. "Who Daniel is . . . was formed in that house. They made my brother a killer. He needs it, and I need him."

Kaleb stays quiet. We've never really called out what we do before.

"What we do every year, I do for him. Daniel is my brother. I have and would do anything for him." I make sure to catch Kaleb's eye. "Anything."

"I know," Kaleb whispers again.

"I would kill and die for my brother."

"He knows," Kaleb tries to reassure me.

I shake my head, eyes focused as I turn onto the private road leading to our parents' lake house. "Charlie tells Daniel that people don't know unless you tell them. So let me be clear, Kaleb . . ."

I slow the car to a stop and turn to the man who became my second brother the minute Helen and Christopher Cromwell brought him home. "You are my brother, Kaleb. You always will be. Whatever you decide, no matter what choice you make concerning her, we will always be family."

Kaleb stares at me, his panicked look almost comical. I stare at him and watch as he takes in my body language and expression.

After a few minutes, he blinks rapidly, and I know he realizes how serious I am.

I don't want him to feel even more uncomfortable. No one likes to be watched when you're at your most vulnerable, so I slowly steer the car down the long, narrow road again.

"It's not right." Kaleb's words are low and soft like he didn't want to speak them. But there's no room for embarrassment in this truck. I've watched this man hunt and gut another human being for sport. Right and wrong have no place here.

"Who says what's right?" I ask. "You do. Your house, your life, your rules."

He nods to show he's listening, but I need him to hear me. I confess my own secret. "I've been fantasizing about killing that college kid for the past several hours simply because he knocked Lara down. Who the fuck cares about right or wrong?" I stress.

The cab of the truck stays silent until the house comes into view.

"Always?" Kaleb asks quietly, his uncertainty clear.

"Always," I promise.

Kaleb moves in his seat, the atmosphere in the truck shifting with him, both relaxing.

My playful brother is back.

"What if I fuck Lara? You know, since you're not willing to go there."

His words hit their mark. My head shoots around to him. "I'll cut you into tiny pieces." The truck swerves for a moment before I'm forced to look away and regain control of the vehicle.

The jackass just grins in my passenger seat. I changed my mind. I only need one brother.

I pull the car over behind where Kaleb's Audi sits abandoned with the back door open. The sight of his prized possession parked so shitty makes me smile, and my own mood lifts.

I lean back against my door and very obviously eye him up and down. "Tiny pieces," I repeat. "Starting with your cock. Although it's already tiny, so cutting it off would have to suffice."

Kaleb laughs, his whole body shaking. "I'll have you know, no one has ever complained."

"Some people don't know any better." I shrug.

His hands start to fumble with his belt.

"What the fuck are you doing?"

"Defending my honor." He laughs.

My chuckle joins his. "Put your cock away. No one wants to see that," I tell him.

"Lara does," he taunts me.

I pause halfway out of the truck. "I always thought it would be Daniel who punched you in the throat first . . . but it's gonna be me," I tell him.

My words don't deter him. They only make him grin wider.

"Let's rescue my princess." He nods at his ditched car. "Then we'll go get yours," he offers, pointing at the house beyond, his words no longer teasing.

I return his smile with one of my own.

CHAPTER SEVEN

Lara

My whole body shakes, pulling me from the edge of sleep, when a cold breeze whooshes around the inside of the car. It's still dark outside, but it's different now, less intimidating. Maybe because I know it'll be getting light soon.

Coldness has seeped in deep, leaving me exhausted enough to rest a little while I wait for someone to leave the house and notice I'm out here. Either that or I'll be out here long enough that I can walk home.

I glare at the open car door, but like the last ten times I've looked at it, I just can't muster the strength to get up and close it.

After clambering back into the car, I curled up on

the back seat facing the open door and haven't moved since. My teeth may be chattering, but my ankle and upper body are still throbbing.

The sound of tires crunching against the ground perks my spirits, and relief floods my body. I don't even know who it is, but all of the stress and pain of the night hits me all at once.

I blink back tears. A car door closes and then another. Two male voices float over. I don't even care who it is. I just need help.

I open my mouth to call out, but nothing happens.

A blurry figure walks around the car, another close behind. Just as the second person reaches out to close the back door on their way past, they do a double take.

Kaleb!

My breath leaves me with an audible whoosh.

"Hi," I croak out.

If I wasn't so fed up, I'd laugh at the way his eyes widen and his jaw drops.

"Michael!" he calls out, his voice a few pitches higher. "Lara."

"Yeah, yeah," Michael answers, coming closer. "Enough about Lara. My patience only goes so far, Kaleb."

Anything else he planned on saying gets lost when Michael rounds the car door and sees me. For the first time since meeting them, it's easy to believe that they're brothers. While they look nothing alike, their mannerisms mirror each other. Wide-eyed and open-mouthed, they stare as blood drains from their faces, only to appear a second later on their flushed cheeks and necks.

Michael recovers first.

"Princess, what are you doing out here?"

I ignore his question and concentrate on his earlier words. "You guys were talking about me?" But my words are choppy, the cold still stealing some of my breath.

Michael frowns. "Remember, I don't like asking twice, and nothing about this is funny. Why are you still out here?"

Fine, be like that. I pout at him.

"Because you said to stay in the car," I tease.

But Michael's face falls. He goes from worried to devastated in under a second. Shouldering Kaleb out of the way, he places both hands on the seat, slowly sliding them forward until one sits at the edge of the seat and the other under along the seam of the seat, stopping when both are on either side of my hips and he's braced his weight on his elbows.

"Tell me you didn't stay in the car at the end of October with the door open just because of what I said."

He looks devastated, genuinely hurt that he may be the reason I'm out here.

It hurts knowing that I put that look on his face. Swallowing hard, I lick my lips, my mouth suddenly very dry. "I didn't," I tell him, shaking my head.

His eyes immediately darken, and Kaleb lets out a strangled sound, throwing his hands up as he turns away.

Oops.

My eyes fly back to Michael's now stoic face.

"Oh yeah, princess, oops."

At Michael's words, I realize I spoke aloud. *Shit,* he looks mad.

Suddenly, his hands grip my hips, and before I can brace myself, he pulls me toward him. My legs slide on either side of his torso with a mind of their own as I fall back, lying along the seat.

"Ahh," I squeak out in surprised pain.

His face rests above mine, my hands clasped in his above my chest. His body looms over mine, connected at only our hips with my thighs encasing his. My feet dangle awkwardly outside the car. Not knowing what else to do, I wrap my good leg around his hip, and my right leg stays stretched out so nothing can touch my foot.

My face flushes, his hips sinking into me deeper, his arousal large and hard against my nethers.

Michael grins down at me. "That wasn't very nice, princess."

I blush even more and fight a moan as he grinds down into me, a soft gasp escaping.

I push away the logical part telling me to stop and think about what I'm doing. For once in my life, I just act.

"Please," I beg breathlessly as I try to pull my hand from his. "I need to touch you."

"No," he snaps.

My face falls at his harsh words.

"No," he says again, much softer. "Let's just move these out of the way, shall we?"

As he speaks, Michael grips both my hands with his right and pushes himself up more with his left braced on the seat beside my ribs.

I don't get a chance to protest or warn him before his large hand brings my arms above my head, shoving them into the seat. All traces of arousal leave me as soon as my hands hit the seat and my shoulder is stretched.

My cry is loud and pain-filled, my discomfort obvious. It's not like before when he pulled me down. That pain was easily overshadowed by what his body made me feel.

No, this hurts. My shoulder is screaming. Michael releases his hold and jumps away from me. In my rush to release him from my legs, my injured ankle catches on the car door, ripping another cry from me.

"Fuck!" Michael stares at me, wide-eyed and panicked. "Kaleb." He calls his brother over.

The minute Michael's body is replaced with his brother's, I want the seat to open up beneath me and swallow me whole.

Why can't I die?

"Please kill me," I moan through my right-hand fingers, covering my face.

"I think my brother has other plans for you," Kaleb jokes. I spread two fingers enough to glare at him through the gap.

"Kaleb!" Michael growls, kicking the closed driver door. "Is she okay?" he demands.

The man above me turns slightly to look at his brother, who stands close to the car door, leaning left, then right, trying to get a better look at me.

"Well, if you'd let me check, we'd know. And don't kick my fucking car!"

Michael scrubs at his face, then gestures as if to say "go on, then."

Kaleb turns back to me.

"Hi." He smiles, but there's something underneath it. He's just as worried as his brother. "While normally I'd understand a woman crying while she is under my brother—"

"Fucking dick, I will punch you in the throat."

"While that's understandable, if not expected," Kaleb continues as if he wasn't just threatened, "that sound you made wasn't normal. You're in pain."

I nod even though it wasn't a question.

"Why?" he asks gently.

Unlike his impatiently pacing brother, Kaleb waits quietly as I blink up at him, tears spilling over.

"My shoulder and my chest," I whisper, tilting my head toward my arm resting above my head.

Kaleb nods, eyeing it thoughtfully. "You didn't fall on your shoulder earlier."

"No," I confirm.

Again, he waits for me to elaborate in my own time. "That sister of yours is a menace."

Both men freeze.

"She drives like she's on a race track. We hit the tree coming around the corner, and the seat belt hurt my shoulder. My ribs, too," I tell him, pointing in the direction we came from.

Kaleb's body drops at my answer but barely makes contact with mine before Michael hits him.

"Did you just punch me in the ass?" Kaleb shrieks.

Michael ignores the question and instead demands, "Get your body off hers!"

Kaleb doesn't move. "My brother just punched me in the ass," he tells me like he still can't believe it.

"Tiny pieces, Kaleb," Michael growls.

I don't understand the words, but Kaleb clearly does as he planks his body over mine, making sure no part of himself touches me.

Back on track, he gestures to my prone arm with his chin. "Can you move it?"

"I'd rather not."

Tears fill my eyes at the idea of enduring that kind of pain again.

Maybe I can just stay here? Shrivel up and die of humiliation.

Like he can read my mind, Kaleb gives me a reassuring smile. "You're okay, Lara. I'm not going to let anything happen to you. Michael," he calls out, "you going to let anything happen to Lara?"

"Fuck no!" Michael answers immediately. "Why would you even ask that? Does she think that?" the large man asks, still trying to peer into the car over his brother's long frame.

"Here is what's going to happen," Kaleb says loud enough for the other man to hear but without taking his gray eyes off me. "I'm going to go to the other side and help support your shoulders as you sit up. Michael's going to bring your arm with me."

"Nuh-uh," I hum, shaking my head.

Kaleb raises his brow. "I wasn't asking, Fawn."

I frown at the nickname and the sweet way he said it. I thought he tried to insult me with it earlier, but now, with the way he's looking at me, it feels kind of nice. Like the big brother I never had.

I swallow the lump that forms in my throat. It's been a long time since someone cared enough to protect me. Maybe that's why I didn't freak out earlier when Kaleb joked about Michael stalking me on my runs. Even as a joke—because that's what it had to have been—it's nice to pretend someone cares.

Lost in thought, I miss Kaleb exiting the car.

Michael positions himself over me with his knees on either side of my hips. Gently, as if I'm made of glass, he lowers my right arm, tucking it at my side and trapping it with his knee.

"Let's keep that hand there, shall we?" I feel his hands moving under me to cradle my shoulders, his face hovering just above my own.

"No, I don't want to. I can stay here until it's time to go home," I stammer out.

Both men ignore me, communicating with each other instead.

"Check her shoulder and ribs before we move her," Kaleb suggests.

Michael tilts as he braces his body on his left arm, his right hand hovering over my throbbing shoulder.

"No, no." I panic.

Michael's face appears above mine again. "It's cold, you're in your fucking pajamas, and you've not stopped shivering."

"I'm okay," I insist. "See, not cold, no shivering." I smile, forcing my body to still for just a second. My teeth chatter as I speak, showing my lie.

"Your nipples say otherwise, princess."

I don't even look because I can feel them. I have zero doubt both men can see them pressed against my robe although Michael seems to be the only one looking.

"I'm going to check your injury, then we're going to get you up and into the house, where you'll warm up in a nice hot bath, then bed."

Both men nod at each other in a silent signal.

Michael's fingers probe my shoulder while his cheek touches mine. His deep voice rumbles against my skin. His words of encouragement are lost, drowned out by my cries.

But it doesn't deter him. He continues to press and poke at the sore skin of my shoulder, moving to my collarbone. Michael doesn't stop, not until I wiggle my good arm free and attack him with my right fist.

His body pulls back as far as he can with the roof above us.

"You okay, brother?"

Michael nods, his chest heaving.

His pained look makes the fight leave my body.

"Easy, Fawn." Kaleb's words break through. "Michael's just doing as I asked."

"It's your ass I need to kick?" I hiccup.

Michael chuckles, seeming to have recovered. He presses a kiss to my temple, then takes hold of my clenched hand and raises it to his mouth, placing a kiss on my knuckles. His fingers entwine with mine, then rest together on my chest.

I consider biting his other harsh fingers that poke at my ribs just as he pulls away.

"Nothing broken," he announces.

Well, no shit!

"I could have told you that if you had asked," I grumble, still breathless.

"Behave," Michael warns. "Don't think I didn't see those teeth." He chuckles.

Shit, I roll my lips over my teeth. I didn't realize I'd actually moved to bite.

Cheeks flushed, I give him a cheeky smile, one he returns quickly.

"I like a little biting, Fawn." Kaleb interjects, winking at me.

"Tiny pieces," Michael says again. Something tells

me those two words have significant meaning because, again, Kaleb reacts instantly. This time, he just rolls his eyes, giving his brother a look that says "really?"

"She has visible bruising. You might want to take her to see the doc," Kaleb advises, pointing at the exposed skin of my shoulder.

"Will do," Michael agrees.

"On three," Kaleb warns.

"Wait," Michael rushes. "I can't." He shakes his head. "I . . ." His words trail off, his voice shaky.

Tilting my head, I witness the look that passes between the two brothers. Neither says anything more, but a second later, Kaleb replaces Michael.

I miss Michael's body instantly. It's irrational and mental even, but I can't help but feel disappointed when Kaleb's left hand grips my right. His other hand slides to my lower back, ready to support me.

Unlike Michael, he stays outside the car instead of leaning in to help.

Catching his brother's eye, Kaleb starts the countdown again. "One." My stomach clenches. "Two." My breath puffs out fast and loud. "Three." My eyes squeeze close as I maneuver into a sitting position. A yelp escapes my mouth as Michael curses behind me.

Nausea floods me, and my head spins, but I sit up with both arms down and my hands in my lap. I blow out a slow breath, mimicking Kaleb, who now crouches in front of me. At least until Michael comes behind him. He grips Kaleb's shoulder and tips him backward out of the way to replace him.

"You did so good, princess," he praises, brushing stray curls from my face.

I give him a watery smile, and my eyes flick behind him to where Kaleb is spread out on his back.

"You're okay," he whispers in a way that makes me think he's trying to reassure both of us. "You're okay," he repeats, bringing my focus back to him. I nod, wanting to calm him too, something he senses. "Tell Kaleb how hard his car hit the tree. It'll make me feel better."

My wide eyes flit between the two men.

"Go on, it'll make you feel good too." Michael encourages with a grin, as Kaleb climbs to his feet.

Huh, I guess Kaleb isn't the only playful brother.

"Oh yeah." I smile. "We bounced off that thing."

Kaleb groans, bends over, and braces himself against his knees.

Michael's right. I do feel better. The man in front of me knocks under my chin and chuckles.

Still laughing, he says, "Let's get you in the bath, princess." His hands rub the outside of my thighs.

My body heats at the firm touches, but he's quick to move away the minute I lift my own hands.

"Kaleb . . ." The name comes out as a plea, one I don't understand until Kaleb steps forward to wrap his arm around my waist and help me out of the car.

I hop awkwardly a few times, trying not to aggravate my ankle even more. Kaleb taps my side and lifts me easily into his arms, my injured shoulder safely tucked into his chest.

After a few steps, he asks, "So why are you outside, again?"

"Your crazy sister left me out here. I tried to go in, but I couldn't make it."

"Name-calling isn't very nice," Kaleb reprimands, looking down at me.

"Neither is your sister's driving," I sass.

"I'm going to kill her," Michael snaps. "What the fuck was she thinking?"

"She wasn't. She was just super mad, I think. I almost opened the door, tucked, and rolled at one point."

"Fawn, you're not athletic enough to pull that off. Besides, Sam's not that bad of a driver . . . I taught her myself," Kaleb boasts.

"Not that bad? Not that bad?" I screech. I have to force myself to take a deep breath, but my inner thoughts still slip out. "I will stab you," I tell him, straight-faced. I feel all self-doubt leave my body . . . I can take him.

A chuckle, sharp and short, bursts out of Michael.

Kaleb squeezes beneath my knee, and my blood pressure rises more. "You don't have a weapon," he reminds me cheerfully.

True.

"Michael." I turn to his grinning brother. "Please, would you get me a weapon? Anything will do. It doesn't even have to be sharp. I'll stab him with a spoon." I squint at Kaleb, but my lips twitch when he throws his head back.

"Stabbing, a girl after my own heart."

I frown at his words. Another one of his jokes, I guess. Maybe he's not so much the funny brother but the weird brother.

Michael's hand wipes at my cheeks again, taking away any remaining frustration.

CHAPTER EIGHT

Michael

My gaze slides to Lara again, unable to look away for too long.

She looks small and fragile in Kaleb's arms. My girl is trying to hide it, but her exhaustion is clear. Her eyelids drop every few seconds, and she literally can't lean any closer to my brother, but at least her shivering has almost stopped.

Jealousy stirs in my stomach, but I know I can't be what she needs right now. The panic and pain I felt when she hit me in the car robbed me of this moment. Thank fuck my brother is here to help.

My fingers twitch to touch her. Rubbing my thumb over my fingertips, I shiver at the memory of her soft, wet cheek.

The thought of why she cried makes my anger rise.

Fucking Samantha.

Clearly, Kaleb hasn't been strict enough these last few years while he's been dealing with her. Perhaps, it's time for either myself or Daniel to step in. A fight for another day.

Who am I kidding? We're just as soft with her.

Looking back at the two approaching the house, my chest cracks open as Lara lays her head against Kaleb's chest, her eyes flittering closed.

It should be me.

Me she trusts, me holding her, and me warming her.

A new level of hatred for my biological parents fills me, and for the first time in the twelve years since Daniel killed them, I wish I had been the one to shove that screwdriver in. Instead, I had stood and watched, fascinated and grateful that my big brother was still looking out for me and more than willing to do what we needed to find peace.

And after a fashion, we had until Daniel needed that again . . . and again.

I breathe easier knowing that the man who sired us is gone, but now it's my turn to be what Daniel needs and make sure we never get caught.

It doesn't hurt that killing is fun.

Kaleb and Lara join me at the front door.

"You okay, bro?"

"No," I answer honestly. Something tells me I'll never be okay while I can't have her.

I reach out, running the back of my fingers over her cheek. It's still cold.

"She's warmer than she was." Kaleb tries to reassure me, reading my thoughts.

"How does a nice hot bath and lots of blankets sound, baby?"

Lara sleepily blinks up at me, all drowsy and cute. "I'm okay. You worry too much," she chastises.

"That's kind of my job in this family."

"I'm not family."

Her words punch me in the gut because in another life, a less screwed-up life, she would be.

Bath and blankets. I nod to myself.

Opening the front door, I stop short. The anger I felt earlier doesn't compare to the rage that bubbles up at the sight in front of me. Samantha is smiling on the lazy chair, a hot drink clutched in her hands, and our parents are snuggled on the sofa.

Lara's foot connects with my back as Kaleb fails to see I'm not moving, and the way my body naturally arches away from the contact, mixed with the pain that sizzles over my skin, pushes me over the edge that I've been standing on since the first day I saw Lara at Duke's.

"What the fuck is the matter with you, little girl?" My question roars across the room. Everyone freezes for just a second, stunned at my outburst, and that somehow pisses me off more.

"Well, I'm glad you can sit here all cozy and warm with your fucking hot chocolate, Samantha, while Lara's outside catching hypo-fucking-thermia." I throw my arm behind me, where Kaleb and my girl are still trapped in the doorway.

Finally, I move enough that they can slip inside to the wood-fire heated room.

My sister's eyes widen at the sight of Lara in Kaleb's arms, as do our parents. Her surprised look turns to a frown, showing their reactions are for two entirely different reasons. It just adds fuel to my fucking fire.

"Get that look off your face," I snarl.

"Hey, now," our father interrupts, his arms out as if banning us to a time-out in the corners of a ring. "Let's calm things down. We don't shout in this house."

"Maybe that's the problem. You baby her. When was the last time Sam actually took a punishment?"

Kaleb shifts beside me.

"Yeah, because shit's always my fault," Sam sasses.

"This fucking is!"

Mom crosses the room when sobs sound around the room, squeezing onto the chair with her baby girl.

But this is one fight Samantha isn't going to cry her way out of.

Kaleb lowers Lara until she stands on one leg like a damn flamingo, forced to lean on the empty couch opposite my parents for support. When she starts to tilt, his hands shoot to her hips to balance her.

I didn't think I could get wound up any further, but I was wrong.

And unfortunately for Sam, she's my target.

"Okay, enough." My father demands, "Sam told us you saw her on a night out and sent her home. As much as it kills me, she is twenty-one years old and can go out with friends. Now, who is this young lady?"

Kaleb laughs at our dad's description of what happened.

"Samantha was caught in the middle of a booty call at the college housing, stole my car, kidnapped Michael's girl, and then had the nerve to leave Fawn outside out in the cold, too injured to come in here," Kaleb explains for me.

My mom's hands still, her eyes rounding at Kaleb's words. My father stands taller as he looks over at Sam.

"Samantha?" he asks, his tone sharp.

"What? Like I don't get to have a sex life." She huffs. "She could have walked in instead of all the dramatics and climbing all over Kaleb."

"She can't walk," I boom, startling her.

Dad closes his eyes and takes a deep breath. "We will deal with your sister."

"Did I mention she hit a fucking tree with his car?" I need them to understand the severity of what happened tonight.

With a raised brow, he repeats, "Your mother and I will deal with Samantha."

"Oh, her ass is mine about that car." Kaleb sneers.

"Fuck you," Sam spits out angrily, tears coming fast and hard, but one look from the normally gentle Helen Cromwell, and she settles back into the corner of the chair, tugging her cover higher. "And fuck her," she mumbles quietly, glaring at Lara.

CHAPTER NINE

Lara

Everyone freezes, shock evident on their face.

I peek at Kaleb next to me, whose brows are shoved so high on his forehead they're practically a part of his hairline.

The first sound is a sniffle, and then a full-on sob rips out of Sam. Not like before, these are gut-wrenching, all-consuming cries. I watch as guilt visibly floods Michael. His shoulders sag, the tension in his body drops away, and his face crumples.

"Fuck," he curses, scrubbing at his face, his distress clear. "Sammy . . ." he starts, but his dad holds up his hand.

"I think that's quite enough, son."

Michael hesitates but eventually gives a firm nod.

"You boys take . . ." He hesitates, not knowing what to actually call me.

"Lara," I fill in as quietly as I can. I don't think I have ever been this uncomfortable.

"You boys take Lara and get her settled for the night." He twists his wrist, looking at the time on his watch. "Well, what's left of it. Your mother and I will talk with your sister."

"A good spanking is what she needs," Kaleb mutters, but his voice carries across the quiet room.

His words only add to the tense atmosphere, and Sam's crying intensifies.

"Not helpful, Kaleb. And we don't hit in this house."

Michael grimaces, rubbing at his jaw.

"Maybe that's the problem," Kaleb replies.

Both parents react to his words. Their mom wraps her arm around an inconsolable Sam, while their dad simply points at the stairs.

Kaleb turns to me, arms out, ready to pick me up, but Michael coughs.

The two brothers share a look with me stuck in the middle. Finally, Kaleb nods once.

"Okay, Fawn, hop on," he tells me. Turning, he crouches slightly and pats his back.

He's joking, right?

"You're joking, right?"

Kaleb straightens, twisting his torso to speak to me. "No?"

"I have a bum ankle," I point out.

"That's why I'm going to carry you."

"I can't hop on." I gesture to my foot again.

"Oh." He smiles. "We've got you." He gestures back and forth between himself and his brother. Again, Kaleb turns away but crouches down even lower this time.

Even as I move forward, I can't help but moan with uncertainty. Hopping, I grasp his shoulders. Just as I am about to do the world's smallest jump, two strong hands land on my hips.

Behind me, Michael lifts me easily, his fingers spreading wide from my hips to the top of my thighs. His thumbs plant on my ass as he grips me tight.

Confidently, he holds me until Kaleb can grab my thighs. Once secured, he stands tall, taking me with him. My face heats when Michael's hands remain for a second more.

I peek over at the other three people in the room. Sam's head is down while her dad quietly berates her. Their mom, however, is not so oblivious. Her steady blue gaze tracks our movement. Something tells me that this woman doesn't miss much when it comes to her family.

Securely clinging to Kaleb, I give a little wave as we pass with Michael close behind.

We climb one set of stairs before Michael passes us on the landing. He climbs the stairs quickly, looking back every few steps, a frown pulling at his face.

"Legs round my waist nice and tight," Kaleb

directs when my hold slips. His hands catch me under my ass before moving back down my legs.

Michael stills in front of us where he had started to lead the way to the top floor. Turning to take us in, he opens his mouth but closes it without saying anything. His face is the same shade my mom went when she found out I gained two pounds at Christmas my senior year. Same cheek twitch, too.

His gaze meets mine before dropping back to where his brother's hands hold me under my thighs, a scowl consuming his face.

What is his problem?

I'm tired of him being hot and cold. One minute, he wants to help me, then he calls his brother over to do it. Now he's looking at us like we stabbed him in the back. Frustrated, I ask the question out loud.

Kaleb stills beneath me, one foot on the bottom step.

Pivoting on the top step, Michael towers over us. "My problem? How about you shouldn't have been out there freezing your ass off in the middle of the night? How about you shouldn't have even been in Kaleb's car in the first place?"

Disbelief floods me. "Do you want me to apologize?" I demand. "Fine, I'm sorry your sister drove off with me in the car, but mostly, I'm sorry you put me in the car to start with."

"No." Michael sighs, pinching the bridge of his nose. "Of course I don't want you to apologize."

His well-muscled chest expands, his eyes squeezed

close. The man looks like he's trying to wrangle his last piece of patience.

"I apologize. I'm tired and worried," he says, looking me in the eye. "Would you please go upstairs and warm up in the bath?"

I narrow my eyes before giving them a quick roll. "We're all tired." I pat Kaleb's chest and add, "Come on, Kay, let's go."

The man carrying me quickly shakes his head.

"No?" I ask. I peer over his shoulder to see his face as we ascend the stairs and ask, "What about Leb? Lube?" I chuckle.

Kaleb's laughter makes me jiggle on his back.

Michael freezes, his broad back expanding as he sucks in a deep breath, pausing in front of a door. "He likes to be called Kaleb."

"Kaykay?" I ask as we step onto the landing.

Kaleb is still chuckling as we pass his brother and enter the bedroom. "You're going to get me into trouble, Fawn."

I stroke his chest where my hand lays. "Something tells me you don't need my help for that."

"Very true," he agrees, releasing me quickly back onto the bed.

"Gentle!" Michael snaps.

Kaleb doesn't respond. Instead, he walks into the adjoining bathroom. The sound of flowing water floats out to us a minute later.

"Wait," I call out. "I don't think I can take a bath."

"Of course you can. You need to warm up," Michael insists sharply.

My cheeks flame. "No, I don't think I can." I stress the last word, hoping he will catch on.

He doesn't.

"Princess, I am out of patience. Go get in the bath."

"I can't." Great, now I'm snapping. "I don't think I can step in and out of the tub," I mutter, embarrassed.

"Oh."

Kaleb looks back and forth between us, having caught the end of our conversation. "I could . . ." He stops short at the noise that rips out of Michael. "I'll go get Mom," Kaleb hurries, practically sprinting from the room before I can even protest.

"And drop the fucking nickname," Michael hisses to his passing brother.

CHAPTER TEN

Michael

Closing my eyes, I take a deep breath. My patience is slipping, and I'm not used to that feeling.

Can I spank her and not fuck her after? *No.*

"You're being rude," my girl snaps, tearing me from my thoughts.

Sitting on the edge of my bed with her arms folded and lips pouted, she is the epitome of sexy. My cock twitches as the need to be with her grows every second.

Her brow lifts on one side, and her sweet face swamps with disappointment. She's upset on Kaleb's behalf. Lara defending him rubs me the wrong way. I want her close with my family, but I want to take first place.

Kaleb's eyes are on someone else. It's Lara's attention that concerns me. Dropping my eyes, I drink her in. Slightly disheveled from being carried, her robe has slipped on her left shoulder, the edge of her cream top visible.

It probably matches her pants. Cute and practical, nothing overly sexy, so why is my cock leaking at the thought of her taking off that duck-covered gown?

Bringing my gaze back up, I catch her wandering eye. Lara bites the corner of her lips as her eyes drop lower on my body. My chest rises and falls rapidly at the thought of her gaze being replaced with her hands.

The thought is exciting, erotic, and completely fucking new.

I worried for nothing; Lara craves me just as much as I crave her.

I lean against the doorframe and relax slightly for the first time since we returned from the college campus. "Is that so?" I smirk.

"Yes." She nods. "Kaleb is just trying to help. You should be nicer."

"I should," I agree. "But I won't."

Her lips thin at my reply, and her eyes narrow.

"You know, if you're jealous, then maybe you should have carried me in," she challenges. I grimace but give a small nod because it's not her fault she doesn't know.

Kaleb's words about being honest and accepted tickle the back of my mind, and my mouth opens on its own.

Could she love me the way I am?

No one will love you the way we do, Michael. Words of the past attack me, causing my stomach to drop and take all playfulness with it. They bother me now more than ever. Back then, our biological mother's words as she handed me over to a social worker hadn't meant much. After all, my brother was willing to die for me. I didn't need anyone else.

But I'm not a child anymore. At twenty-seven, Daniel's love isn't all I need.

Closing my mouth, I stay quiet. My eyes roam over her form as she leans back.

Her bottom lip pouts out when I don't respond.

"Fine." She shrugs. "If you don't care, maybe Kaleb can help me in the bath after all."

I push off the doorjamb before she's even finished her words. My body looms over hers, my knees caging her legs in, careful not to touch her foot. Grabbing hold of her wrists in each of my hands, I use my large frame to coax her flat on the bed. I pin her roughly; I don't want to pull her shoulder again, so I keep her arms low. The sight of her trapped beneath me will be one to play over and over when taking myself in hand.

"Don't ever say those words again unless you want me to fuck your ass raw," I threaten. My chest heaves as I grapple with my last ounce of control.

"I was beginning to think you didn't like me like that, like this," Lara whispers, a smile playing on the edges of her lips, and for a second, I let myself hope.

She's interested, but her body gives away her fear. Her short, harsh breaths are not from arousal, at least not entirely. Her eyes are wide and scared.

"Kaleb will not see you naked," I warn.

"Why not?"

"Because you're not his."

My gaze drops, watching the way she licks her lips, her teeth tugging on the corner of her bottom lip as she debates her next words.

"I'm not yours either."

Lowering my head, I run my nose along hers. The touch sizzles my skin, electric and hot.

"Am I?" she asks, sounding almost hopeful. For the hundredth time since I first saw her, I wish I was different and could be what she needs.

"No, princess, you're not."

Breathing her in, I run my nose down the nape of her neck. She smells like lavender and something else, something that I just can't put my finger on. It fills my chest, catching my breath in the same way that stepping out into the crisp night air does. Winter . . . she smells like winter.

I drag her into my lungs more, gulping in air as if it'll somehow mold us together and make her a permanent part of myself. Nudging away the edge of her robe until I get to what I want, I wet her skin with my tongue.

"If you were, you wouldn't need to ask. You'd know." My words caress the cotton of her thin cream tank top. Her nipples, already beaded, grow harder.

"You will allow my mother to help you in the tub, you will soak until you're nice and toasty, and then I'm going to tuck my princess into bed."

"No, I . . ."

Her words are cut off when I wrap my teeth around her left nipple, biting down on the hard bud.

A yelp echoes around the room before it transforms into a moan, my bite having changed to gentle sucking, my tongue soothing back and forth.

Lara arches her back, her chest following me as I pull away.

"You were saying?"

Lara lies trapped beneath me, panting for a few seconds before answering, "I can't. I don't even know your mom."

Wrong answer.

Lowering myself to her chest, I go for her left nipple again. This time, my bite is longer, harsher.

A breath chokes out of Lara.

"Please," she breathes.

I nip at the hardened bud, and her startled cry fuels me. I watch as her mouth falls open with another plea, but no sound comes out. One more nip gets me what I want.

"Okay, okay," she pants desperately below me.

I raise my eyes but move my mouth to the underside of her breast and suck harder.

"I'll be good," she promises.

Hearing what I want, I tongue her nipple. Lara's

body shivers under me, and her chest arches, craving more of a rougher touch.

I soothe her sore skin through her top. The cream cotton is soaked, her rose-colored skin beneath easy to see. I pepper kisses on her heavy breast, slowly making my way back to the oversensitive skin, laving it with my tongue once more.

I'm gently suckling when a throat clears behind me. Pushing off her, I spring away from the bed while she gives a startled squeak. Sitting up, Lara grips the edges of the blue robe, shoving it closed.

Kaleb stands near the door, grinning. "You might want to, uhh, hide that." He gestures to my straining cock, the gray sweatpants doing absolutely nothing to hide my desire.

No longer distracted, I can hear Mom climbing the last few steps to join us on the third floor. *Shit.*

Walking to the bed, I sit beside Lara, who's dazed and trying to catch her breath.

"Could you shut that off?" I ask him, pointing at where the bath water is still running.

Lara flops back on the bed as Kaleb leaves the room. Her hands fall to her sides, letting the gown fall open again. Reaching over, I rub her belly, an effort to soothe her embarrassment and an excuse to touch her again. Moving up, I tug the robe back to the center of her chest.

Quickly, I slide my hand inside, then grab and pinch her right nipple. "Get in the bath. No arguing."

When she quickly nods, I give her a bright smile,

releasing just as Mom enters my room. "That's my good girl."

Her already flush cheeks darken even further at my words.

I can't hide my grin as my mother enters the room. I guess Daniel is onto something with the whole "good girl" thing.

Crossing my ankle over my thigh, I lean forward to hide how my cock is still trying to fight its way out of my pants.

CHAPTER ELEVEN

Lara

"That's my good girl." Michael's words heat my body, my cheeks flaming even as their mom helps me hop into the connecting bathroom.

Peeking back, I see Kaleb take my place next to his brother, both men raising a brow at my hesitation.

Seeing no other way out, I close the door. My forehead taps the wood at the same time as it clicks closed.

Blowing out a sigh, I try to regain control. I need to get ahold of myself. Since when do I go to second base with strangers and let them grope me while their family is nearby? Never. I guess there's a first for everything.

"I have a daughter and three sons. At this point, there's not much I haven't seen. There's no reason to be embarrassed. I'm not here to judge or make you feel uncomfortable."

The sweet words help ease some of the tension in the room. Turning the best I can, I give her a grateful smile.

"Plus, my mother-in-law lived with us for a few years toward the end. My husband, Christopher, hadn't wanted a stranger helping her with day-to-day things. So bathing was my job." Her words help. The woman also screams calm and collected. "Unless of course, it's the make-out session you just had with my son that has you blushing like a schoolgirl." She smirks with a raised brow.

Not so much making out, more letting her son do some heavy petting. Not that I'm going to correct her.

The hot room suddenly feels like a sauna. Her laughter echoes around the room, and she closes the distance between us until she gently pats my over-heated cheeks. Her kind blue eyes roam over my face, taking it in for just a second. A few pieces of her shoulder-length hair shimmer in the light, the blond and white strands mixing as it falls from behind her ear.

Blinking away tears, she says, "I'm so glad he found someone. I pray they all do, but after Daniel met his wife, I worried Michael might . . . struggle. I had hoped my next daughter-in-law would walk into this house of her own accord, but maybe Kaleb's girl can come here without being carried." Her words end with a chuckle.

Seeing my confusion, she brushes my hair back away from my face. "Ignore an old lady. And in case my smitten son didn't already say, I'm Helen. Or you can just call me Mom."

My jaw drops at her words. "Oh, no." I shake my head. "Michael and I aren't like that," I insist, but my words lose all credibility when the wood beneath my back jolts from a forceful knock.

"Mom, is she in the bath? Princess, remember what we talked about."

"Didn't talk much," I mutter.

Helen takes my elbow, supporting me to the vanity.

"Michael, do you want to come in here instead, or are you going to leave us girls to it?" his mom demands.

There's a slight pause on the other side of the door. "No, ma'am."

I smile at such a large man being chastised by a woman Helen's size. Winking, she nods at the bubble-filled bath. "Let's get you in."

CHAPTER TWELVE

Lara

Sighing, I melt further into the hot water. Even after what must have been a good thirty minutes, the hot bath still soothes.

I hadn't even realized how cold I was until I lay down. Bubbles up to my chin, I'm slowly losing the fight to stay awake. Even the pain in my shoulder, ribs, and ankle has receded.

"How're you doing in there?" A voice sounds through the door, disturbing our peace.

Rolling her eyes, Helen lifts her head from the magazine she's been flicking through, sitting just a few feet away.

After the first few embarrassing moments of a stranger helping me undress, where I prayed the floor would collapse and take me with it, having Helen in here hasn't been so bad. Plus, it somehow helped when she told me she'd helped Charlie, her daughter-in-law, bathe after she'd given birth to their first grandchild.

"No, I drowned her in the bathtub, Michael. I'm just cleaning up the crime scene."

The door immediately opens, showing a panicked Michael. Concern is etched all over his face as his wide eyes frantically take in the room.

His face darkens when he sees his mother perched on the closed toilet lid and me almost entirely submerged.

"You're not funny." He glares.

"I'm also not incompetent." Helen tuts, going back to her magazine.

Suitably chastised, Michael gives a cute smile. One that tells me Kaleb isn't the only charmer in the family.

Glancing up, Helen scrunches her nose at her son, returning his smile. "You can leave us alone now, dear."

"She should get out now. She'll prune soon."

Helen glances at her watch. "You go on and head to bed. I'll help Lara."

Michael hesitates, rubbing at the back of his neck. "I . . ." He struggles before dropping his hand. "I want to tuck her in."

My stomach flutters at his words.

"You're a sweet boy, Michael," Helen whispers, ducking her head, but it's not hard to see the way she blinks quickly.

"So?" Michael asks, tilting his head back toward his bedroom.

Helen doesn't bother to look up from where she's reading her article. "When she's good and ready. Not a moment before." This time, she does raise her head, her emotional gaze finding mine. "You ready, dear?"

"Nope." I smile at her. Lifting my injured ankle out of the water, I wiggle my toes and roll my foot.

The room stays quiet, so I lift my head. Helen has gotten lost in her reading, while Michael's eyes are fixed to where my leg just disappeared.

"What?" I blush.

"Nothing." He grins. "Well, nothing I'm going to say in front of my mother."

"Michael!" Helen and I chastise him at the same time, not so lost in her reading, I guess.

The three of us are smiling as he squeezes his large body out of the bathroom without opening the door any more than he has to.

Kaleb's probably still with him.

I bite my lip. Maybe it is time to get out.

"I should probably get out," I say, sitting up.

"You sure? Don't let him rush you. Besides, it never hurts to make a man wait." She grins.

I laugh at her words. "I'll try to remember that."

Standing, she moves, the towel waiting on the vanity. "He always has been a charmer, that boy. Had to be, I guess." Her last few words barely float over to me, muttered so low.

In the mirror, I catch sight of her wiping away a stray tear.

"I'm so glad he found you." Her voice wavers, and our eyes lock in the reflection. "He's the baby I always worried about. Sam is social and outgoing. Kaleb, well, he was a troubled teen, but he was older than Michael and Daniel had been when they first arrived, and he knows people. He's cheeky and charming. Daniel doesn't need that kind of love, at least not before he met Charlie. But Michael . . ." She shakes her head.

Sniffling, Helen wets her lips. "Michael's whole world is his brother. He loves us, and I know that, but Michael's whole life has been about filling a debt and caring for Daniel however he could."

She turns, giving me the same soft look as when she cradled my face earlier. "I just wanted more for him."

Just like earlier, I tell her, "We're not like that."

"You will be."

I don't argue because I'm not sure what Michael and I will be after tonight.

"Let's get you out of that bath so your man can tuck you into bed, huh?" she asks, shaking out a large bath towel.

Her words nudge at me until I can't help but say, "I'm not sure he wants to be my man."

Leaning my hip on the counter, I slowly dry off

one-handed while Helen rubs the end of my hair, gently running her fingers through the damp strands as she goes. "He's never brought a girl home before."

"He didn't bring me. Sam did."

"True." She nods. "Something her father and I are punishing her for," she adds quickly.

And Kaleb will. But I keep the thought to myself.

"I have known Michael since he was seven years old, yet I've never seen him look at someone the way he just did. Never heard one of his brothers refer to someone as his girl either."

"That was just Kaleb joking." I shrug.

"Maybe," she agrees, helping me step into some red pajama bottoms.

"Why else would he ask Kaleb to carry me up here and not do it himself?"

Pulling the tank top over my head, I don't sense the shift in the room until I see Helen's face.

Her lips have thinned, and she won't look at me. Instead, she fusses with the towel, releases the tub plug, and lets the water out.

"Helen?"

Her whole body stills, her back facing me. "It's not my place."

"Is it something I need to know?" I ask, panicked. This woman was just insisting her son was interested. Why has she clammed up now?

Wrapping her arm around my waist, we slowly make our way to the door. Just as she's about to open it, Helen pauses. "Michael doesn't like to be touched."

I frown. "He touched me." Hearing how that sounds, I rush to add, "Before I mean, outside."

Helen shrugs. "He can give small touches but nothing big, except with Daniel. Those two have a bond like it was forged in hell. And I guess it was."

He didn't carry me because he couldn't. My heart breaks at the idea of what could cause a man to be that way. And I'd taunted him.

We step out of the steamed bathroom. Michael and Kaleb are instantly on their feet, like they've been worried we couldn't manage.

Michael stands a few inches taller than his brother, but the width of his body catches my breath. Michael is broad. His biceps strain against his jacket, and the T-shirt does nothing to hide his muscled chest. Everything about his body is evenly proportioned to match his height.

The man is perfect.

My eyes dip lower, my mind bringing back the feel of his body looming over mine. I can't help but wonder if it really is proportioned everywhere. From what I saw earlier, I don't think that will be an issue.

God bless gray sweats.

Kaleb is muscular but somehow still slim, like some of the other runners I see. He might be smaller than his brothers, but he is still above average height. His bulk might not hit you in the face like his brothers', but I felt his strength earlier when he carried me. Kaleb hadn't struggled, and it was hard to ignore how his abs rippled as he brought me into the house.

"All warm and clean." Helen smiles.

"Perfect," Michael says, his possessive gaze rolls over me, scanning my face first. His eyes drop to my breasts, down over my good leg, to my bare toes, and back up to my chest. His attraction is clear, so why does he keep pulling back?

Helen's words ring through my head.

Michael's watchful eyes take me in again.

My body reacts to his appraisal. My breasts grow heavy, my nipples beading fast. The thin cotton does nothing to hide them.

Worrying his lip, Michael gestures for Kaleb to help. Lifting me off my feet, he carries me across the room, placing me gently on the bed next to where the covers have been folded back.

"I'll leave you kids to it, but the pair of you get to bed soon," Helen tells her boys. "We've all had enough for tonight. Breakfast will be at noon, so sleep in."

"Thank you," I tell her.

Her eyes flicker between myself and Michael. "You're very welcome. Anything for family. That's our motto."

I blush at her words.

Turning, I slide my feet under the covers, careful not to catch my tender ankle. Kaleb leans over to pull the covers farther up the bed.

"I got it," Michael tells him, pushing off the set of drawers and walking over.

"Night, sis." Kaleb grins, pressing a kiss to my forehead.

"Kaleb," Michael warns, but then turns his furious gaze to me, and his face softens immediately. "Lie back."

Turning away from Kaleb's retreating back, I do as I'm told.

"How are you feeling?" Michael kneels beside me. The fingers of his left hand skim my shoulder, making me shiver.

"Better."

His large hands squeeze my hips before tucking the covers tight to my body. "As snug as a bug."

Satisfied I'm not going anywhere, he folds the top of the cover so that it sits under my chin.

My eyes drop to his mouth, my breath coming quicker.

Softly, the back of his fingers brush over my cheek, the same cheeky smile as earlier taking over his face. His thumb wipes over the skin of my forehead where Kaleb kissed me a few moments ago.

My heart flutters when he replaces Kaleb's kiss with one of his own.

"Good night, princess. I'll be next door in Daniel's room. If you need me, just shout."

Swallowing the lump in my throat, I just nod, unable to speak.

His large body stills in the doorway, illuminated by the hall light. I can just make out his sad expression when his face turns back into the dark room. "I wish I was different. That I was better, but I'm just not."

Somehow, I know he's talking about more than just a good night kiss. Disappointment consumes me, and for the first time tonight, I cry.

CHAPTER THIRTEEN

Lara

I loop the lace and pull it through the other, tugging until the knot is nice and tight. The sneakers fit perfectly. I feel a little bad about taking a pair of Samantha's shoes, but Kaleb was right. It's the least she can do.

Besides, I'll drop them back in a few days, along with her laundered clothes. I cringe at the memory of her dropping the clothes into Michael's room earlier. Awkward was not the word. Kaleb loitering behind, listening in, hadn't helped.

But at least the leggings and T-shirt fit . . . just about. I shrug on Michael's jacket, the large size making me feel less self-conscious as it swallows my body. Sniffing the collar quickly before anyone can see, I smile when his cologne surrounds me. How can he make me feel this safe when I only just met the man?

Rolling up the sleeves, I roll my eyes because I need to get a grip. Tugging the borrowed shirt down again, not that it helps, I stand from the stairs.

"Princess, come have breakfast, and then I'll drive you home," Michael calls from the kitchen table.

"Oh, that's okay. I can run back." I insist, despite the slight limp I have as I join them in the kitchen.

Michael's head snaps to me. "The fuck you will," he tells me, twisting to look at me over his shoulder.

His words irk me. That, coupled with my anxiety about not doing my usual morning exercise, makes me stop short and snap, "Excuse me?"

But he doesn't back off. Instead, Michael turns in his seat, his body facing me full on, and doubles down. "Princess, it's not happening. You're lucky I've let you walk at all this morning."

"Let me?" I huff, my mouth dropping at his words. "I wasn't aware that I needed permission. And I'm not asking. I'll run back."

"No, you won't." He shakes his head. "Say it a third time and see what happens." His face sets in a blank stare, and something in my lower tummy flutters.

I open my mouth to do just that, but his face darkens, and something inside me takes over. Survival, maybe. Whatever it is, I swallow the words, glaring when he smiles at me like he just won.

Because he did.

Jackass.

Helen shifts at the counter. "I'll make you something, sweetheart."

Stepping into the kitchen, I shake my head. "Thank you, but I don't normally eat breakfast."

"You should," Michael reprimands me. The man's been in a sour mood ever since we came downstairs.

"Leave the lady alone, son. The first rule of dating is to know when to pick your battles." The older gent sits across from Michael. He gives me a playful wink as I pull out the seat beside his son.

"Dad."

I don't need to see his face to know Michael is exasperated. Christopher seems very happy to annoy his son about the possibility of having a girlfriend.

"What?" He grins. "I'm just having a bit of fun I missed out on in your high school years."

Helen's words from last night take root in my mind. I guess it's hard to have a girlfriend if you can't be touched.

Is he a virgin?

I feel a thrill race through me at the idea of being the one to teach him, of sharing that with him. But one look at the way his eyes roam my body as I settle into my seat, I know I won't be his first.

I guess he found a way . . . just one his mom doesn't know about.

"What time is everyone coming for the movie

night this Sunday?" Helen joins us at the table, gathering plates and cups into a pile.

"Oh, I can't." Kaleb shakes his head. "I'm driving one of the trucks for the timber yard. Leaving tonight."

"Again? Can't one of the other drivers go?"

Kaleb shrugs, grabbing another muffin. "It's a heavy load. Plus, there's nothing to stay for. Something tells me this Halloween will be just as quiet as last year." He and Michael share a look.

Shit, do they know about the party at their campsite?

A loud clang startles me.

Helen leaves the plate where it fell, the ceramic chips littering the end of the table.

Straightening, she stands behind Christopher, her hands settling onto his shoulders. "Chris, tell the boys they need to stay here this weekend."

"They aren't boys anymore, Helen," he tells her, patting the back of her hand. "Daniel and Charlie are joining us here, so you'll have Belle. Sam will be here, too."

"Nuh-uh," Sam mumbles around her muffin. "There's a Halloween party on Sunday."

My eyes bulge at her words. There's only one party I know of, and this is the one table it does not need to be announced at.

"You're grounded," Christopher reminds his daughter.

"I'm twenty-one."

Their dad opens his mouth to argue more, but Kaleb beats him to it. "Old enough to be arrested for grand theft auto, assault with a deadly weapon, and just being a general pain in my ass."

Her lips pinch. Kaleb's lucky that looks can't kill.

I slouch further into my seat, not wanting to be seen. My mom and I go at each other's throats whenever we're in the same room, but this sibling rivalry is a whole new ball game.

"Grand theft? It was your fucking car, and I didn't assault anyone." Sam points a finger at her own chest.

Kaleb points down the table toward me. "You hit her with a tree."

So much for not being seen.

Michael sits up straighter beside me. "Yes, you did."

"The road was slippery, and I was in the car, too, not that you care. You two are the fun police."

"That's what happens when you drive like a moron," Michael adds.

"Oh, and I have fun." Kaleb sneers. "It just doesn't involve jumping on the nearest college dick."

"Hey!" both their parents yell.

My eyes widen. *Holy shit.* Breakfast with my mother doesn't seem so bad right about now. *No, I take that back. Nothing's that bad.*

Reaching over, I snag the piece of muffin trapped in Michael's hand. His eyes flit to me, then back to his now empty hand.

Blueberry, meh. I thought it was chocolate chip.

He doesn't say anything, but his hand drops to my knee, giving it a small squeeze. My insides melt. The small gesture means so much more for him than I'll ever understand.

Silence settles over the room, no one willing to break it first.

I'm thinking about sneaking out when Michael stands and pulls my chair out too. "I'm going to take Lara home."

I give the room a small wave. "Bye."

Kaleb scrubs his face. "Bye, Fawn. Don't be a stranger."

"Bye, Lara. Make sure you keep your promise and go see the doctor in town if you're still in pain tomorrow, please," Christopher tells me. It's not a question.

Maybe his boys get their demanding personalities from him. It's always the quiet ones.

"Do you need Kaleb to carry you out to the car?" Michael whispers.

I shake my head quickly. The worry on his face wipes away my annoyance at his earlier words. He's just worried. "I'm feeling better, not one hundred percent," I admit, honestly. "But I'm okay. I'll go to the doctor if I need to," I promise again.

His eyes search my face. "You better," Michael warns after a minute.

So bossy.

The large hand on the small of my back makes

my thoughts fall away, but even distracted, it's hard not to notice the shift in the room at Michael's action.

Stepping into the living room, I glance back to see Helen give me a bright smile.

"What are you blushing about?" Michael asks as we step out into the cold air.

CHAPTER FOURTEEN

Lara

Loud music thumps around me as our bodies grind together in the dim light. Candles, oil lamps, and flashlights litter the sides and floor.

"Are you sure the Cromwells won't know we're here? Their cabin is, like, right down the road," I yell to be heard.

Cassie shrugs. "Darrell says they're not there tonight."

I roll my eyes at my best friend since junior high. *Oh, if Darrell says.*

"That boy barely knows his own name. We could get kicked out of college for this," I insist, glancing around.

Handing me a beer, the blonde throws her arm around my neck, dragging me toward the back door and into the open air. "They won't care. Besides, you can just suck that middle brother's dick, and he'll forget about the whole thing."

Why did I tell her about Wednesday?

"The man didn't even give me his number. He's not interested." I pout.

"Ahhhh!" a large masked man yells. He jumps out from the side of the house with his arms raised.

Cassie and I both scream. She lowers her arm and shoves me toward the masked man while I throw my beer bottle at his chest.

Darrell rips the white mask off, doubling over with laughter as relief and anger flood me.

Dick. Head.

"You should see your faces," he says, still laughing. I hate him.

"Baby, you scared me." Cassie slaps at his stomach, but she doesn't even sound angry. Her hand roams over his chest, then up and around his neck. "We're going to need that mask later."

I think I just threw up a little.

"Whose cock are you sucking, other than mine?" Darrell asks. I shiver as he looks over me, and the cold air has nothing to do with it.

"If by suck, you mean bite off, then sure. Right after you find it, but I hear it'll take a while." Two of the guys closest to us laugh at my words. The real dumb and dumber, Brian and Oliver. Never too far from Darrell.

Their leader sneers, pulling an oblivious Cassie

closer. "Maybe next time you see that mask, I won't be jumping out from around a corner."

"What are you, five?" I snap, pointing at the discarded mask.

Darrel pulls his mouth away from Cassie's long enough to reply, "No, because I wouldn't be about to fuck my girl if I was."

I don't try to hide my disgust at his words. The man's repulsive and a dumbass to boot.

Cassie might be my best friend, but her taste in men sucks.

His hands grab and squeeze her ass while I'm standing right next to them. His eyes meet mine at the same time his lips latch onto her neck.

Wanting to be anywhere else, I head to where the keg sits, manned by a trio of footballers. Looking down, I step over his creepy mask. The white stands out in the darkness of the night, but it's the bright red lips that freak me out.

As I glance around the crowd, three more of the same masks stand out in the darkness. They put me on edge. Ever since the clip of the Halloween killer wearing one was leaked earlier this year, the guys at college have been obsessed with getting their own for this year's Halloween.

Sadistic assholes.

Tonight is not going to end well. This whole party was a bad idea.

CHAPTER FIFTEEN

Michael

"That's the prick from the campus parking lot. The one who shoved your girl down," Kaleb tells me, pointing at the broad guy wearing a number twelve football jersey like I didn't notice. I send my brother a look.

But aloud, I say, "She's not my girl."

"Well, why didn't you say that last night? I wouldn't have minded her riding me until dawn."

He wants me to kill him.

"Is this how you felt?" I ask, turning to Daniel.

"Yes," he answers, still looking down at the summer camp through his binoculars.

"I'll never flirt with Charlie again," I promise him.

"Charlotte." Daniel corrects me, still hating her nickname.

"This is why I don't do relationships." Kaleb laughs.

"Why are you here?" I glare.

"The timber yard is behind schedule, so I can't take the load until Tuesday. My brother from another mother, you get the pleasure of my company for two more days."

"It's not your company or your pleasure he wants."

My head shoots back like I've been slapped. "Daniel Cromwell, did you just make a joke?"

My big brother grins at me.

"If Charlie asks, you're at Kaleb's house?" I ask about his alibi.

"If anyone asks, we're all at my house. Alcohol and cards," Kaleb pipes up.

My mind rolls back to the last time we needed an alibi. "Cooper still being a pain in the ass?"

Kaleb chuckles. "The fuck face formally known as Officer Cooper, is running for a spot on the town council."

"The man still thinks he's the police," Daniel adds.

"The man's a joke," my younger brother says.

"He is." I nod. "He's also the only one outside of family who knows what we are. Show the man some respect."

"I'd like to show him the end of a shovel."

Daniel grunts in agreement.

I'm the odd man out. After the stunt he pulled

with taking Charlie and the restraining orders, it's probably not an argument I'm going to win. Who knew getting rid of a restraining order would be so hard? If I ever hear the words "processed means processed" again, it'll be too soon.

Talk about taking your job seriously. We had to wait weeks to get it lifted, only to find out that Charlie had gone home to her family.

The man deserves what's coming. But one of us needs to be the voice of reason. "The man's too close to kill. Give it enough time. His life is falling apart, and our dad has made him a town pariah. He'll kill himself eventually."

My brothers share a look. "We'd rather do it," they echo.

What are they, fucking twins?

A commotion at the back door draws our attention . . . Lara. Number twelve jumps out, scaring my girl.

Okay, so maybe she is mine.

Wearing a replica of my mask! The only person who gets to terrify her with that is me.

"He dies tonight." I don't even know when I stood, but I can't just sit here and watch. My body twitches with the need to kill something, to watch as he struggles for his last breath.

"Err, you might want it to be him." Kaleb points, offering his binoculars.

Lara stands near the keg, chatting with another girl. It's not her who Kaleb is pointing at. Behind her, another jersey-wearing prick, number nine, fills a red plastic cup with cheap beer . . . and a tiny pill.

She can't drink that.

I'm panting before I even start running. Rage fills me to the core. Never have I understood the term seeing red as much as I do right now. Because that's all I want. His blood everywhere.

"The girl with the curly hair, too, take her drink," Daniel calls after me.

But it's too late. Even from here, I can see the other girl lift her cup to her mouth, taking a small sip.

Lara smiles her thanks, then takes her own drink.

I'm almost there.

Pulling down my mask, I stagger out of the woods with my eyes locked on Lara, too rushed to be careful of the forest foliage.

My appearance startles everyone, including Lara. My nervous girl drops her drink, and the alcohol spills out, seeping into the soil quickly.

"Fuck, dude, that was good. You got us good," the kid at the keg says. A dead man talking.

"Mine was better," their little leader says, walking over with his arm around another girl. "It's always better when you make a pretty girl scream." His arm might be around someone else, but his eyes are on Lara. No, they're on the mess at her feet, and he looks pissed.

Why the fuck would he care if she didn't drink her beer? Motherfucker.

We're killing four tonight?

Still fueled by adrenaline, I reach out a gloved hand and take hold of Lara's. Towering over the jock, I stare at him through the eye holes in my mask until he swallows, moving out of the way without a word.

Pussy.

Everyone else has gone back to dancing, if you can call some of this dancing. I'm pretty sure the two near the tree line are fucking.

I want to reach out my other hand for the girl who has already drunk some of the spiked drink, but my tongue feels swollen at just the thought of touching someone.

The heat of Lara's small hand in mine reminds me that I can. *I guess it just has to be the right person.*

Just like they always do, one of my brothers saves me. Kaleb walks out of the trees, hockey mask in place. He does a double take at the couple grinding against a thick tree. Within seconds, he's beside me, taking charge of the other girl and guiding her into the cabin.

Lara and I silently follow.

Once in the cabin, I don't know what to do. This isn't something I've ever done.

Releasing Lara's hand, I glance around. Candles, beer bottles, red cups, and trash are scattered throughout the kitchen.

It's a mess.

But the sight is a welcome one. Memories of Halloween two years ago fill the room. My rage starts to fade, and my cock twitches at the thought of what happened here.

Kaleb bends low, whispering to the other girl. The music swallows his words, but I know he'll take care of her. We're killers, not animals.

"Umm, do you want a drink?" Lara shouts, drawing my attention.

I shake my head. This mask is definitely not coming off. I point at her, asking if she does.

My girl nods, her hair slipping over her shoulder in a thick braid. She looks pretty, her large jacket covers her upper body, but her ass and legs look perfect wrapped in tight jeans. The black sneakers make me smile.

Grabbing a bottle of beer, I move around the kitchen, searching for a bottle opener, but I don't see one. Bracing the lid on the edge of the counter, I hit it quickly to knock it off.

"Clearly not your first time." Lara laughs. "Making good use of your college years, I see," she flirts.

I don't respond, unsure of what to say. "I never went due to the anxiety of leaving my brother" doesn't exactly have the right ring to it.

I cringe under my mask.

At least she's flirting. Even with me masked, she feels the pull between us.

Lara's smile drops, seeing Kaleb lead her friend out of her room. "She's fine," I say. Lara jumps. It could have been the voice modulator on my mask or the hand I slide inside her open jacket to rest on her ribs, but I don't ask to find out. "He'll take her home. The cups were spiked," I tell her.

But that only makes her worry more.

My hand slips away, and for the first time ever, I miss the warmth of touching another person.

We step out onto the porch when red and blue lights color the dark sky.

Daniel.

Not wanting to get caught out here, especially in this mask and outfit, I loop my arm around Lara's waist, lift her, and jog into the woods.

The air whooshes out of her lungs.

She feels small and fragile in my arms as I run, ducking and turning for several minutes until the lights of the party and the police are nowhere in sight.

Happy we're a safe distance, I set Lara down. She turns on me as soon as her feet touch the ground.

"Where has he taken her?"

"I don't know," I answer honestly. "Probably home."

"And I'm supposed to believe that your friend will just take a drugged girl home and not hurt her?"

"Yes."

"No!"

She turns, taking a step in the camp's direction. That's not happening. The cops are there, and so are those college kids.

Footsteps start approaching, so we need to move. Gripping her hand, I turn her to me. "No," I tell her sternly, the modulator making my word that much sharper.

Her hand pulls, slipping from my grip.

She needs more. Twisting her slightly, I bring my hand down on her ass three times in quick succession.

Wide brown eyes stare back at me in disbelief, like she can't believe I just did that. Funny, me neither.

Our eyes lock, but I refuse to back down first. The footsteps get closer, and finally, Lara blinks quickly.

Biting her lip, she takes my outstretched hand, her shorter legs moving quickly to keep up as I guide her deeper into the woods where no one will pass us trying to rush back to campus.

Once hidden in the forest, our walk turns slow, silent, and comfortable. Maybe the small spanking she got was enough of a reprimand that she now hates me. Not that Lara knows it's me under the mask.

My heart hammers in my throat when the college campus peeks through the trees. I don't want my time with her to end. Stepping out of the woods, I keep my hold on her hand as we cross the main road.

The closer we get to the building, the more my resolve is tested. I don't want to let her go.

But I can't put it off forever, no matter how slow we walk. At the building entrance, Lara turns to me.

"Thanks for walking me home, big guy. Sorry I gave you trouble."

I nod, and Lara's lips twist like she's debating something. She doesn't leave me waiting for long. Reaching up, she braces herself on my shoulder. My whole body tenses, ready for the pain to hit, only it doesn't.

Too stunned, I almost miss the way she presses a small, sweet kiss to the side of my mask.

"The whole mask thing is kind of growing on me too." She rolls her eyes.

"Go straight to bed," I order.

"Yes, sir." She grins.

And with those two words, my resolve crumbles. Standing alone in the darkness, I watch as my girl heads inside, turning to give me a small wave.

My girl.

That's what she is.

My princess.

CHAPTER SIXTEEN

Lara

My breath pants out of me. Arousal pulses through my body, settling between my legs.

Groggy, it takes me a minute to take stock of what woke me. My earmuffs are gone. Music from the party fills the room obnoxiously loud. The downside of living in college dorms? The floor parties.

I must have slept fitfully because I never sleep on my stomach. My eye mask is gone, too.

Jesus, how long has the party been going?

Blinking, I look at the red numbers glaring at me from the bedside table, 2:47 a.m. I've only slept for a little over two hours? No wonder I feel exhausted.

Still blurry-eyed, I push up onto my elbows and knees, or at least I try to. My forearms are barely near my head when something tugs on my wrists, and large hands settle on my hips, pushing them back down.

My heart stops. It wasn't a dream. Someone's in the room with me!

Everything comes into focus all at once, the way my arms have been laid out above my head, the ribbon is soft but restrictive as it wraps around my wrists. My inner thighs are coated in my arousal.

My scream rips through the air, but it's swallowed by the music. No one outside of this room can hear me. My body shakes, fear and arousal warring when a mouth lowers to my overheated pussy. Big hands spread my legs farther apart until he settles between them. His grip lowers so he can bend my knee, and my back arches, giving him better access.

My body has a mind of its own.

The man behind me does not let up until I'm crying and on the edge. His tongue alternates in its attacks, swirling my nub, then shooting down to stab inside of me as far and deep as he can go. I don't even know who is eating me out, but he's acting like his life depends on it, like his next breath hedges on me coming.

He won't have to wait long.

My mind forgets that this is wrong. My body responds like it wants him more than it wants air. My breath jams in my throat as I climb higher and higher.

This can't be happening. I can't let this happen . . . Can I?

I'm on the edge of doing more than just coming.

Swallowing a plea for more, I press my lips together tightly.

Reaching my arms above my head, I feel for the bars of the headboard where the ribbon is tied. My fingers clutch it tightly, giving me leverage to pull myself up the bed and away from him.

Something he doesn't appreciate. His hands are much harsher this time when he pulls me back down the bed, a solid force as it strikes my bare ass.

A warning.

My face heats as the spank makes my pussy spasm. I've never had this reaction with a boyfriend before, not even when we have tried things a bit rougher.

I moan, my hips lifting. His hand strikes me again, his palm hitting the same spot over and over. Harder and harder until I lie there whimpering.

Another warning . . . I'm not supposed to enjoy my punishment.

"I'm sorry," I sniffle.

Something wet and soothing rolls over the heated skin of my ass . . . his tongue.

And I'm moaning again. I need to see him.

"Please," I beg.

The bed shifts beneath me as he crawls up the mattress. His hand is rough, his grip harsh in my hair as he shoves my face into my pillow.

Hot air pants along my cheek, making my body shiver. I've never been this close to an orgasm without sex before.

His hips push into mine, and his cock, thick and hard, grinds against my sore ass cheek. He pulls his hips back, settling between my legs.

This is it. I'm about to let a stranger fuck me in the darkness of my bedroom. A man I've never met before. A man who just gave me the best oral of my life. A man who I wouldn't recognize on the street.

Scream for help. But even as the thought occurs, I brush it off quickly because I don't want to. I want him.

His clothes brush my ass and the back of my thighs . . . he's fully dressed.

Reaching between us, he grips his cock, nudging my entrance.

"Please," I beg again, wanting to see the face of the man about to fuck me.

His chuckle sends shivers down my spine. The hand between his legs moves, and I hear shuffling near my face, like he moved something.

Confused, I wait.

The grip in my hair turns me to face the left, where my full-length, freestanding mirror is. A car passes by my window on the parking lot outside, the lights illuminating the room at the same time I catch a glimpse of us in the mirror.

My face is flushed, arousal obvious. But it's his face that makes me scream. A white mask with red lips hovers over me in the mirror. His head tilts, and I just know that beneath the mask, he's smirking.

Terror fills me at the same time he does.

I buck against him, but it only shoves him in deeper. The force of his thrust knocks the wind out of me.

My orgasm rolls over his shaft.

My hands grapple to steady myself, fearing I'll hit the metal headboard, but his grip on my hair pulls me toward him, arching my back.

The room is filled with the sounds of his moan and my gasp. The bed strains under us, the metal whining in a desperate plea as the ribbons refuses to give way.

With each gasp, I drag air in through my mouth that's so thick with our arousal I can almost taste my own wetness.

His cock, thick and long, makes me feel full. Stretching me in ways I never thought possible. The feel of his open trousers caught between our bodies is erotic and speaks of his need to fill me so quickly he didn't bother to strip.

But it's not the cock that's inside me that bothers me, it's the man attached to it. Everyone who wore a mask tonight flashes through my head. I buck again, trying to dislodge him, but he's buried too deep.

"Please, don't be Darrell."

The man above me freezes, his body turning to stone.

"You ever say another man's name while my cock is inside you, I'll go out and kill everyone with that name, just to make sure I got the right one," he hisses.

The way his body looms over me and the power

124

he exudes, I believe him. His hand comes down on my ass with an unforgiving slap. The force is so hard I shift forward, his cock slipping out a little.

My heart floods with relief despite the threat. It's not Cassie's boyfriend. His voice is mechanical, altered somehow. Just like the masked man at the party, the one who dragged me away when the cops arrived.

The one whose friend brought Stacey back to the dorm and forced her to lock the door, only leaving after she promised not to open it to anyone. No matter what.

I'd been beyond worried when I got home earlier. I had snuck onto her floor, needing to know she was okay. And she was. Terrified but okay. Without breaking her promise, she'd explained through her locked bedroom door how her own mystery man had lectured her the entire way back about the risks of accepting drinks from anyone. Of what could have happened.

I didn't feel much like partying after that. With a quick good night to anyone I crossed paths with, I went straight to my dorm room, crawling into bed even more thankful for my own masked man.

I hoped to see him again. But I hadn't imagined it this way.

"No," I whine as he moves back, pulling his cock out.

Metal clangs, and I think he's undressing more at first, but the feel of the warm leather coming down on my ass extinguishes those thoughts. He rains it down over and over until I lay flat on my bed, sobbing into my pillow.

My ass feels like it's on fire.

"You don't ever say another man's name," he tells me again.

I nod quickly. I lie still, hoping he won't leave. His panted breaths fill the room so loud that even the music's bass doesn't drown them.

"I'm sorry," I tell him, needing him to know. "I won't. I'm sorry."

He doesn't speak, and eventually, his hips settle against my sore ass. I brace myself just in time. The thrust of his cock is quick and hard.

Buried deep, we stay still, just happy to be joined. I'm splayed out, my hands wrapped around the bars of the headboard and my legs spread wide. He leans over me, his left arm bracing him beside my head, his right hand once again buried in my hair. His upper body looms, not touching me, but it somehow makes it feel all that more desperate.

And then he starts to move.

Fuck. Me.

I knew it would be good. Rough and unforgiving like the man himself. But nothing could have prepared me for the way he takes my body. Thrust after thrust, he goes deep, painfully so.

My body grips him for dear life. I'm moaning loudly. The sound of skin hitting skin competes with the wetness of my arousal. Just as I'm about to peak, he stops.

"No." My moan is long and whiny.

I'm practically panting, begging for more, but only when my body calms does he push back in.

By the fourth time of him doing this, I'm physically shaking, tears wetting my face.

"Please," I beg again for the millionth time. "I need it."

His chuckle just makes me cry more, my shoulders sagging.

"What do you need?"

I pause for just a moment, not wanting to say the wrong thing. I can't take him doing it again.

Wrong move.

His movements start again, and I pray he'll let me come. It's painful, the sex, the denial, knowing what I'm doing with him. All of it hurts, yet it's the best sex I've ever had.

His hands bunch my pajama shirt, gripping the top and the bottom together, in the middle of my back. The hold gives him leverage to yank my body back and forth.

I pant, trying to tilt my hips, anything to just push myself over the cliff. He stills again.

"Bad girl."

"Please," I sob into the pillow. "You."

"What?" he demands, pulling my hair to the left of my face.

My neck screams at the angle, but it doesn't

matter. Nothing but coming matters. "You," I scream out. "I want you." My words end on a sob.

"That's my girl."

His right hand lands on the mattress, and he pulls almost all the way out. I know this time will be different.

"Yours." I nod.

I feel his body tense and close my eyes in anticipation, my arms lock to take the force of his thrust . . . but it doesn't come.

The doorknob to my room rattles.

"Please, ignore it."

He doesn't. A soft pat to my ass, with a quick and serious, "Quiet," is all I get as my masked man climbs off me, then the bed.

I lie helpless and needy.

The doorknob jiggles again. Panicked, I tug at my restraints, pulling left and right. I only work myself up more when the ribbons don't release.

A hand settles on my right ankle, startling me. His forefinger wiggles across the sole of my foot.

"Shh."

Can I trust him? Something tells me that I can, probably the same part of me that says to let a stranger fuck me. But right now, I don't have much of a choice.

Sucking in a deep breath, I try to calm my racing heart and start to close my legs.

He huffs, tapping my foot sharply.

He can't be serious? The handle wiggles again, and male laughter floats in.

Someone is about to come in here. I'm spread out and bound to the headboard. Humiliation floods me . . . along with a fresh course of arousal.

I'm beyond wet.

Someone is breaking into my room for the second time tonight, and I'm so wet anyone in the room can see how much the thought excites me.

"Shhh," a male voice whispers. "Don't wake her."

"Not until he has her where he wants her." Another laughs.

How many of them are there? The door cracks open.

Where's my masked man?

I squeeze my eyes closed.

"Look, just bring the party down this hall and set up outside so no one hears."

My breath catches, and I recognize that voice. Darrell.

Stretching my neck, I peer over my left shoulder at the door. His large form slips inside. Light spills in for just a second, but it only shines into the bathroom, leaving me and the rest of the room in darkness.

He turns, his back facing me, and fist-bumps his friend through the gap in the door. My eyes fill with tears.

Quietly, he closes and locks the door. Stepping out of his sneakers, his hands drop to his pants button.

I whimper at the sight.

Darrell's head shoots up, his eyes widening at the image of me spread-eagle on the bed.

My mouth opens in a silent scream, seeing the white mask appearing behind him. Slowly, the dark form of the taller man creeps forward. Dressed in all black, the mask seems to float, stopping right behind Darrell.

Oblivious to the danger, Darrell's eyes drop to my bare pussy the same minute a baseball bat passes over his face, quickly pressing against his throat from behind. The masked man holds the bat on either end, using the leverage to keep Darrell in a chokehold, the wood unrelenting against his neck.

The two men grapple, but my man is bigger.

They stagger to the left toward the door. The masked man tucks one end of the bat into the crook of his elbow, his other hand pulls the opposite end toward himself, pressing the bat tighter and tighter on Darrell's neck.

Darrell's face is growing redder the more he's robbed of air. His eyes bulge, his hands clawing, desperate to live.

My eyes are glued to them, unable to look away. Darrell can't win this; he didn't come in here for a good reason.

Did your man?

Did he? Is waking up with him eating me out any better than Darrell sneaking in here? I shove the thought away. What we've done tonight, I've wanted that. Even as I screamed and thrashed, I griped and pleaded for more.

The two men fight a foot away from my bed, yet my legs stay splayed apart because he told me to. He hasn't forced me to do anything.

The two fall into the door. *Shit, will his friends hear?* But only banging and cheers come from the other side.

Assholes.

Darrell and my man stumble away from the entrance farther into the room. That's when I see it. The playful way he moves.

My man's not worried. While Darrell gasps for air, he's toying.

That knowledge settles something in me, a peace I don't think I should have while two grown men fight in my bedroom as I lay helpless.

Tackling Darrell to the ground, my man forces him to his knees. "You see that?" the mechanical voice asks, his finger pointing at where I am. "That woman, that pussy is mine."

I both cringe and flush at his words.

"What did you come in here for? Hmm?"

Darrell doesn't answer. A gurgle escapes his throat. His head is ripped backward by his short brown hair.

My man really has a thing for pulling hair.

"Were you going to crawl into bed with her? Force your disgusting dick inside her?"

My eyes fill with tears at his questions. It's true.

Darrell has no other reason to sneak in here and need his friends to cover for him.

"Baby, are you watching?" he calls out to me.

I strain to see over my shoulder more. I can only stare helplessly as the larger man steps back and flicks the bat off the floor with his foot, catching it in his right hand.

He twirls the wood once, twice, his eyes meeting mine in the darkness. Light coming in through the thin curtains shows me his blue eyes, our gazes locking across the small room. Then he raises the bat and turns to a bleeding and breathless Darrell before bringing it down. Over and over, the wood hits its mark.

My stomach roils, and I gag. I'm grateful when Darrell falls back with the first blow, taking his body out of my view.

But there's no escaping the sound. Wet and blunt, the bat hits him over and over. Not being able to take anymore, I bury my face into the pillow.

"Look at him," the voice behind me roars.

Crying, I shake my head. *I can't.*

Something wet splashes over my back, causing me to sob harder. I don't need to see to know what it is. The smell of copper replaces the smell of sex.

Finally, the blows stop.

I try to see what he's doing, but when I look back, I only see how his mask lights up from the light coming off his cell phone, splashes of red covering the white. A drop of blood drips down onto the already red-painted lips, the color blending like it belongs there.

His tapping fingers makes me frown.

Who the fuck could he be texting?

My face falls onto my pillow again, the cotton wet from my tears and snot. Hot breath pushes back into my face with every shudder that falls from me.

My crying continues, never stopping even as a gloved hand snatches the pillow beside me. A nudge to my hip encourages me to lift so he can put it beneath me. The pillow is thick enough that my back arches. My ass sits slightly higher, my knees steadying my lower body.

My body shakes as sobs roll out of me, and he lines his cock up. We moan together as he eases back inside me.

The movements that follow are just as forceful and unrelenting as before, maybe even more so.

I cry because Darrell is dead, I cry because the man who killed him is fucking me, but mostly, I cry because I don't want him to stop.

My muscles clench tighter than before. Still sensitive from his earlier teasing, my body is eager to return to where we left off.

His hip movements don't stop. He sneaks his hand beneath me, seeking out my trigger button.

And when he finds it . . . I fly.

A scream rips out of me, and heat floods my nethers, liquid gushing out. And pleasure consumes me.

"Holy fuck," he pants as his cock leaves me.

His hands tap my ass. "Let me back in, baby," he groans. The broad head nudges me, but I'm too tight. I've never come like this before. My leg muscles lock, and my body shakes uncontrollably.

Heat keeps pouring out of my pussy.

He tries to push into me again, but I'm still coming.

"Shit, I'm nearly there." His knuckles graze my ass as he beats off, trying to find his own ending. "My cum's going nowhere but inside you. One way or another."

His meaning doesn't register, not until his hands spread my cheeks. The head of his cock breaches my virgin hole before I can even say no.

His cry mixes with mine, my pain with his pleasure.

My head is yanked back, his hand around my throat, the other in the crease between my thigh and my hip.

"Look at us, my cock in your ass, my cum inside you," he taunts. His blood-splattered mask rests next to my flustered, sweaty face in the mirror.

My empty channel squeezes, searching for him. Our eyes locked in the mirror. I stare open-mouthed as my body takes him over and over.

The crown rubs something inside me just right as it moves back and forth. His cock slips deeper as his cum eases the way. He's not even halfway in back there, and it feels so full, too full.

It only takes a few more motions to send me flying again.

Coming down from the best high I've ever felt, I give a final cry as his body leaves mine.

I lie panting as he climbs from the bed, moving about the room.

Sound to my left makes me turn my head, a smile on my face. But it's not him, it's not my masked man. Instead, it's another.

A huge man, even bigger than my own, stands beside my bed. His face is hidden by a hood-like mask made of burlap.

I scream, short and sharp.

How long has he been here?

His head tilts, like he's taking in the scene on the bed, then he gives one strong nod, and a deep mechanical voice says, "Shower, clean yourself and her. I'll sort out here."

My man replies, "Start with the bed and the wall behind. We haven't finished for the night. I've missed the thrill of killing. No more skipping our hunt nights."

How had I forgotten that the man whose essence drips out of me killed a man not twenty minutes ago?

The new guy nods his agreement.

Hands touch my shoulders, rolling me onto my back. The mask that excited me so much earlier now looms over me in a terrifying way.

"Let's get you in the shower, princess."

Princess.

The word rattles around in my head, my wrists dropping free one at a time until I just lie there with my hands on either side of my head, unsure what to do.

Princess.

It can't be.

Confident fingers move down the front of me, opening one button, then two, then three, all the way to the bottom.

The sides of my pajama top are pushed wide. The memory of him doing the same to my legs earlier makes my body heat, and my nipples bud as air hits them. His finger brushes over one, then moves to enclose my other breast in a large hand, squeezing and rubbing.

"Shower." He nods to the connecting room.

I shake my head quickly. He needs to leave, and I need to call the police.

A sound clangs on the other side of the bed, and the other man freezes. Shit, I said that aloud.

My man's hands brush the side of my breasts, his grip on the open top enough to pull me until I'm sitting up.

"Princess, we're going to take a shower where I'll wash your body, then mine, before bending you over and taking your pussy again. Then we'll come out here back to bed, where I'll fuck you at least three more times. However many it takes for you to know that you're mine and for me to know that you'll feel me inside you all day tomorrow."

Princess.

"Michael," I whisper.

His hands brush the hair away from my face, his mask inches from my lips.

The smell of copper and sweat makes me lightheaded.

"That's the only name you say in bed from now on. Until death do us part." The words start harsh, the mechanical voice rough and scary, turning to a soft whisper, spoken into my mouth as his lips touch mine, the mask falling discarded onto the bed.

Wet with my tears, our lips mold together. He's forceful, taking everything I have to give.

My lip quivers after he frees me, but he quickly sucks it into his mouth. A reminder that I'll never be free, not now.

There is no denying, no forgetting what happened here tonight.

Across the room, Darrell sits on the floor. If I hadn't witnessed what happened in this room, I'd never know who it was. He's wrapped in plastic like he's been fastened up with a giant roll of cling wrap.

His body is propped against the wall, facing the bed. Had he been put there like that before or after Michael climbed back onto the bed? Had he posed his body to watch us?

My stomach roils, and I double over as I gag.

Encouraging me to the edge of the bed, Michael pushes my head low. "Take some deep breaths. It'll pass."

The other man, Daniel by the size of him, sprays something onto my wall. The smell of bleach burns my nose.

Michael's brother stands on the bed, scrubbing the wall behind it.

The bedroom light flicks on, leaving me naked and bare to their eyes, my top left on the bed while I stand.

My steps are shaky, a mixture of shock, horror, adrenaline, and the remains of the best orgasms I've ever had.

Michael's words of what will happen now somehow heat me. Even now, walking past a dead body, wrapped like a giant fucking present, with his older brother in the room, I crave this man.

He's a killer, and I want him.

I eye the bedroom door, and the party is still booming on the other side. A gentle kiss lands on my shoulder, then another. My feet stop, and I stand between the two doors.

Blunt teeth sink into my left shoulder, painfully pinching the skin.

Pivoting to the left, I enter the bathroom.

I can do nothing but stand and watch as Michael opens the shower door and turns the water on. Steam fills the room quickly.

My hiccuped cries are interrupted by the rustling of his clothes as he strips. Carelessly, he leaves everything in a pile at his feet.

The smell of copper is stronger in here. His

clothes are black, the blood soaked into the dark material remaining hidden from the naked eye.

A hand that killed a man not too long ago is now held out in front of me. I ignore it.

I hate him. I hate myself.

But I need to wash off the blood that I can feel dried on my back and the cum that drips out of my ass.

His ignored hand spanks my ass as I pass.

"Don't be disrespectful, Lara. This is happening. You have all night to accept it."

I'm crying again, not that I ever really stopped.

Michael joins me in the small shower stall but makes sure his body doesn't touch mine.

How had tonight gone so wrong? It was supposed to be just a silly party. A night to have fun.

Happy fucking Halloween.

His fingers scrub and scrub. His hands turning me this way and that. I don't fight him because I want nothing more than this night to be washed away.

I glance down at the plug hole. The water is rose red, almost pink as it swirls down the drain. Michael didn't have blood on him since his clothes protected his skin.

My shoulders shake.

Me, the blood is coming off me. Seeing it is so much worse.

Forceful hands tilt my head back, one under my chin, the other holding the back of my head steady as he moves me back under the spray.

The water quickly washes away my tears. Together they mix, leaving me along with any remaining fight.

I'm exhausted, physically and emotionally.

I let Michael maneuver me some more, willing to just let him take charge. By the time he's done, I have my hands braced against the tiled wall, my body folded at the hips, my legs shoulder width apart, ready to accept him for the second time tonight.

With a scream, I take him into my body, knowing that he's right.

I am his.

CHAPTER SEVENTEEN

Michael

I leave the bathroom tired but satisfied.

The cleaning solution stings my nose, but I'm used to it.

Lara stumbles slightly as she steps into the bedroom, her whole face scrunching up in the most adorable way.

The room is clean and sterile, the body gone. Buried, I'm sure.

The bed is made, new bedding and a blanket where the old bloodied sheets and quilt had been.

Steadying her, I take Lara over to her bed as Daniel climbs back through the second-floor window like he's not a six-foot-seven giant of a man whose shoulders barely fit through the frame.

I raise a brow to check we're all good. His mask

moves, and I laugh, knowing he's giving me a raised-brow look as if to say *does this look like my first time?* His arm reaches out, passing me some rope.

Lara sits on the edge of her mattress, her head shooting up when the rope touches her wrist. "No, no. I'll be good," she promises, frantically trying to move farther onto the bed, but she doesn't get far.

Catching her under the knee, I tug her back to the edge, looping the rope around her wrists quickly.

I wish I could trust her word, but I saw her face earlier. She meant it about calling the cops. She's not getting a moment without me for the foreseeable future. Not until I'm convinced that she's all in.

I tie her to the headboard with enough length that she can turn and lower her arms in her sleep. I want her secure, not uncomfortable.

She proves that she's made for this, made for me as she lays there pliant, blinking up at me. Her cheeks and eyes are dry but red. I roll her to the side. Her face flashes with pain as I bend her legs at the knee.

Pride fills me. Neither time was I gentle with her.

The knowledge that no one else has breached her ass before excites me, and my erection is back in full force by the time I crawl into bed behind her.

"Shhh," I soothe. "You're such a good girl, my good girl." I praise her.

Daniel chuckles from across the room at my choice of words, and I smile but don't look at him. Instead, I sink myself into my girl. Her inner muscles are wet, hot, and sensitive along my cock.

Lara whimpers softly at our bodies joining. Her body pulses, growing slicker with every second.

Rising onto my elbow, I memorize her face as my hips repeatedly hit hers. Hard and rough. That's who I am. I won't apologize for that, nor will I change it.

She's mine—her mind, body, and soul.

I've taken one. She'll have no freedom until I take the other two.

She whimpers below me. Her mouth drops open, forming an *o*. Her hands grip the rope, which is knotted just above her hands.

I fought this for as long as I could, but now I'm all in. Whether she likes it or not.

Her pussy squeezes at that moment, showing me we both feel this pull between us, and as my brother moves around in the bathroom, cleaning up the mess we made, I let myself fall, releasing into her at the same time I release a prayer into the universe.

Let it take root; let her give me the family I want.

CHAPTER EIGHTEEN

Lara

For the second time within a few hours, I wake feeling groggy and confused. The digital alarm clock beside my bed screeches, letting me know it's eight-thirty.

Two groans fill the air.

Michael reaches over me, knocking off the alarm. His hair is mussed, his eyes heavy as he kisses me. Our lips move together lazily, and the small spikey hairs on his cheek tickle my skin. I squirm, the weight of his arm on my waist and the pain between my legs drawing me further out of sleep.

The man hadn't been joking when he'd said I'd feel him all day. It's like an imprint of his cock was made as far deep inside me as he could get.

My inner thighs feel raw; the skin is chafed and

still sticky. My muscles scream, and pain shoots from my thighs to my crotch, making me flinch.

My eyes widen at the memories of what we did last night. The sex while his brother cleaned the room, the repeated fucking Michael gave me, breaching my ass. The man he killed.

Life will never be the same, no matter what I do.

"Stop," he tells me sternly, a sweet kiss to the side of my head taking away some of the bite his word carries.

I nod, biting my top lip. I do as he says and stop pulling at the rope. It wasn't giving way anyway. My breath shudders out of me, but I have no more tears left.

A small pulse jumps behind my right eye. I need water, painkillers, and coffee, and not in that order.

I bring my hands down to my chest. "Please?" I motion to the rope keeping me in bed.

Michael ignores my plea, his arm tightening around my waist.

I turn my head toward him and whisper, "I need to go to school."

His brow rises, his eyes assessing.

But it's not a lie. I do have class.

Michael smirks, his fingers teasing as they lower the blanket. "You could always call out sick." His body moves closer but stops, leaving a little space between us. Head bent, his next words are whispered into my neck. "You do sound hoarse. Not that I'd expect anything less with all that screaming last night." I can feel his smile.

Shame fills me. I had screamed for him, screamed for more. Begged, even.

I pull away quickly, staggering to my feet. The rope keeps me planted close to the bed, my back hunched slightly.

The early morning light hasn't quite started to come through the drapes, leaving the room shrouded in shadows, yet I have never felt more exposed, not even when he was devouring my body last night.

This morning, my mind corrects.

A twinging in my crotch reminds me that barely a few hours ago, we were still rolling around in tangled sheets.

"I can't. I have a test." I lie, yanking on the rope hard enough that the bed frame moves.

"Stop," he orders sharply, standing quickly. "You'll hurt yourself."

I'm already hurting.

Gentle fingers soothe the red skin, stroking softly as he releases me.

Stepping back, I remove myself from his touch, practically sprinting toward the bathroom.

"Lara," Michael calls, "One day soon, you'll find out what happens when you're dishonest with me."

My throat bobs as I swallow my fear. His words hold a threat of violence, and after what I saw last night, fear should be the only thing I feel . . . but it's not. My nipples are beaded, my breasts heavy. My ass clenches, and my pussy weeps.

Quietly, we just stare, our gazes locked.

Finally, Michael relents, climbing back into bed. Running his fingers through his hair, he settles against the pillows.

"Take a quick shower, and I'll drive you to school."

What? No!

I need space and time to think of how to fix this.

My mouth opens to say something, anything. But one look at his face and my words evaporate.

I quietly head into my bathroom, hating how, after everything, I still take in the way his bicep bulges, how defined his six-pack is, and how much it bothers me to see those small silvery scars that litter his torso as I shut the door.

CHAPTER NINETEEN

Michael

Lara is hiding in the bathroom. I glance at my watch again for the second time in as many seconds. Her first class of the day starts in an hour.

I glance at the open laptop. She really should have a password to keep strangers out. Anyone could open it and access her schedule, not that I need it to know she's a liar. The woman's terrible at it.

The bathroom door finally creaks open.

Alarm and relief play out on her pretty face when she sees me sitting on the edge of her bed.

Her robe dips, leaving a tantalizing vee of skin for my eyes to devour, which of course I do.

"I laid your clothes out for you." I nod to the small pile beside me.

Lara hesitates. "Are you going to shower?"

I hold my arms out in invitation, creating room for her between my knees. When she's close enough, my hands settle onto her hips. "No." I shake my head. "I want to smell you for the rest of the day."

A cute gasp fills the air. I find it adorable that that's what scandalizes her.

Another flash of flesh draws my eyes lower, and like a man starved, I dive in.

My nose brushes her soft feminine flesh, and my tongue reaches out, searching for her moist lips. So caught up in getting another taste of her, I don't see her hands move until it's too late.

They feel heavy like bricks settling onto my shoulders. She doesn't have to push me away because I practically dive back onto the bed.

Eyes wide, gasping for breath, I crawl backward into the middle of the bed, needing distance between us.

"I'm sorry," she croaks, her hands raised like I'm a wild animal. If only she knew . . . last night was just the tip of the iceberg.

I can't speak. Instead, I just nod toward the clothes.

Out of guilt or maybe it's fear, Lara loses her robe quickly.

Taking a deep breath, I inhale her body. Red marks litter her pale, creamy skin, acts of last night branded on her skin for a few more hours.

The sight makes my balls ache with the need to fill her and brand my girl in another way. My eyes zero in on her smooth flat stomach. Other than Lara herself and peace for my brother, I've never wanted anything more.

Smoothing the dress down over her breasts, Lara glares, probably over the fact that a bra was not supplied.

One less item to take off.

My thought must be written all over my face because Lara scowls. "Really?" she asks, holding up the thick pantyhose.

"It's cold out," I explain.

She rolls her eyes. "So give me panties." After a brief pause, she adds, "Or pants."

I laugh, my smile wide and genuine. All traces of panic gone. *This girl.*

"Quicker to get inside you."

"Yeah, for you and everyone else." Her words are low, mumbled but not quiet enough.

"Repeat that," I dare her.

That kissable mouth of hers drops open. I climb off the bed, intending to use it. My hands pull at my belt when a solid knock on her bedroom door interrupts us before her lesson can start.

"Put the panty hose on," I order, heading to the door. One deep breath, then another, fails to calm my blood.

I'm not mad. Lara's just pushing boundaries,

fighting in any way she can. But I need her to learn that there is no fighting this.

I would know, I tried. But the bond we have, the connection, is just too strong.

She's mine, and I'm hers.

Nothing and no one can change that.

Adjusting the front of my jeans, I wait by the door, my hand flat on the surface just in case, while Lara finishes dressing.

Satisfied she's covered, I gesture to her brush with my chin. "Braid it for me?" It's a question, not a demand.

The clothes are a way for her to follow an order, the hair . . . I just want something to wind around my wrist when I take her tonight.

She thinks her little kitty hurts now; I'm nowhere near done with her. I don't think I ever will be.

That woman owns me.

I debate whether to wait for her to finish as the brush glides through her long, thick tresses after the asshole on the other side of the door knocks again. If you can call that bang a knock.

Ripping the door open, I startle the pricks on the other side.

A laugh booms out of me. *God, I wish Kaleb was here.* What are the fucking chances?

Mr. I Used to be Someone Cooper, as Kaleb now calls him, stands with his arm raised, ready to knock again, mouth open, his eyes growing wider with every passing second.

The girl I saw exit my family's camp cabin with Lara last night stands a few paces behind Cooper with the dead kid's friends.

I can't quell my grin. I knew someone would come looking today after all his friends helped him get in here, but Cooper, he's a nice surprise.

"Is there a reason you're attacking the wood of my girl's door?"

He tries to peer around me, but I'm too broad, and he's too short. But at six foot four, most people are short to me.

"Your girl?" he stutters.

I don't answer, just stare like I think he's a moron.

"This is your girlfriend's room?" he asks again.

This time, I do answer but not for him. Opening the door wide, I give him a clear view into the recently cleaned room.

Standing from where she knelt to tie her sneakers, Lara takes my outstretched hand. My fingers flex, the feeling of holding someone's hand still new and foreign.

"Fiancée, actually."

I hear rather than see Lara's sharp intake of breath, but I don't trust Cooper enough to look away from him. If I'm being honest with myself, I keep my gaze away from her so I don't see disappointment or her rejection.

I'm not asking, I'm telling.

"Since when?" her friend demands.

Lara tugs at her hand, trying to break free of my

hold, but I don't let her. I'm never letting go. Spreading my fingers, I wiggle hers to interconnect them.

"It's complicated," Lara whispers.

Cooper's eyes drop to our fingers.

He smirks. "Another one of those, is it? You Cromwell brothers just can't find someone who wants to fuck you willingly, can you?"

Lara wanted last night; I know that, but his words hit their mark. But cool and calm is my thing. I'm not giving him what he wants. My face doesn't react, even if my heart does.

Why did I ever stop Daniel or Kaleb from killing this motherfucker?

"Why are you here? Shouldn't you be out job searching? I hear no one in this town wants your has-been ass?" Okay, so I can't hide my annoyance completely.

Michael, I warn myself.

No good comes from me losing control. Images of last night and how I filled Lara argue with me. Okay, so maybe losing control has its advantages, but murdering Cooper in a hall full of witnesses gets me nowhere but locked up and away from my soon-to-be wife.

The kids behind him shuffle, looking between themselves. They don't know he's a loser.

"I'm searching for my nephew!" he growls flustered.

"And that's supposed to mean something to me?"

I know what's coming, but this is Lara's first time, so I try to soothe her by brushing my thumb back and forth over the back of her hand.

She remains quiet, a step behind me.

"He came in here last night," the shorter boy yells, unable to contain himself, earning a glare from Cooper.

"No, he didn't." I shake my head.

"The kids say he did."

"And I'm saying he didn't. I was here all night with Lara. Why would another man come in here?"

Cooper doesn't have an answer.

"You're sure Darrell went in?" he checks.

The two little shits nod. "We helped him get in," admits the one with a bruised nose. You'd think he'd have learned his lesson from Kaleb the other night at the fire alarm. He'd be dead if Daniel had punched him.

Un-fucking-believable.

"You heard them," Cooper challenges, like his words mean anything.

"I did."

Leaning against the doorframe, I squeeze Lara's hand. So far, my girl has stood quietly while worrying her bottom lip. I'd like to keep it that way.

"Well then, move so I can look inside."

"No." I shake my head.

"No?"

"I know you're not too bright, Cooper, and it

sounds like your nephew inherited that, but what about me makes you think you're getting inside this room?"

I see it, the moment he realizes. This time, I do fight my smile. It's one thing to beat his nephew to death because he deserves it. It's another to gloat to his face . . . maybe when we finally kill him.

"Your perverted nephew isn't my problem."

"You've met him! Ha!" Cooper points his finger a little too close for my liking.

My right hand releases Lara's to snatch his hand before he can make contact, not too gently shoving his hand away, disgust etched on my face.

"His friends just said he broke in here last night, which he didn't, but if he did, it wasn't for a good reason," I stress. "Aren't you Darrell's girlfriend?" I ask the girl he'd been all over last night.

She looks at Cooper, then nods.

"He's been missing all night," she tells Lara, her worry clear.

"Maybe he found someone else for the night. Doesn't sound like he was a good boyfriend," I suggest.

"Was?" Cooper's eyes grow three sizes. "You did it, didn't you? You killed my sister's boy."

Lara steps away, backing into the room slowly like I won't notice. She's at her limit. Giving her as much of a break as I can, I pull the door close to my side, hiding her in the room.

"I don't know what you're talking about. It's outrageous accusations like that, that cost you a career, Cooper. I said *was* because your nephew's friends just ousted him as willing to spend the night in someone else's room. I'm sure that . . ." I pause, waiting for her to give me her name.

"Cassie."

"I'm sure that Cassie can find someone else."

Cassie nods. "He's kind of a shitty boyfriend."

I gesture as if to say, *there you go then*.

"He's out getting his dick wet somewhere or recovering from a night of drinking."

"How do you know they were drinking if you didn't see them?"

This man really thinks he's slick.

"Because I spent the night in here, with a party going on out there. Anyone within a five-mile radius knew there was a wild party here last night." I smirk. "Besides, it was Halloween. Who doesn't party on Halloween?"

The bedroom door slips from my grip. I hadn't expected it to open from within. Lara rushes past, her book bag in hand.

The crowd in the hall parts like the Red Sea as she whizzes through them.

"Lara," I call, a warning in my voice. She can't outrun this. Outrun me.

Cooper blocks my way as I try to follow her, so I can't pass him without touching him. Grappling to the death is different since I don't have to hold back. At that moment, I'm free to let the pain fuel me.

Fuck!

I track her with my eyes until she's out of the hall. Her keys still sit in the pot on the shelf next to me. I can't leave her room open for Cooper to snoop through.

There's nothing for him to find, but if he touches her belongings, her clothes, her delicates . . . Then I really will have to murder him today.

Keys in hand, I shoot a quick text to Daniel. I'm going to need him at the campus. Having a brother that's head of security for all of my family's businesses is about to come in handy for the millionth time.

I need to leave. Time to end the fun.

"Boys, did you help your friend break in to a female student's room so that he could attack her while she slept, or were you drunk and mistaken?"

"Ignore him, boys. We'll go down to the station and make a report."

That got their attention.

"We thought you were going to take care of it, Kyle?" Bruised nose may have the balls to go against Kaleb with his friends there, but it seems he's not a complete moron.

The two young men share a look. "Maybe we made a mistake." He shrugs. "Maybe he met a girl and went back to her room instead."

"Yeah," the other agrees. "We were pretty wasted last night. Sorry to bother you, man."

"We're done here," I tell them all, stepping out and locking the door.

"You won't get away with this one. This is personal. Darrell's family."

I turn my head and survey him head to toe. "Then you should have taken better care of your family."

CHAPTER TWENTY

Lara

For the first time this morning, I can think clearly.

No bed that holds memories nearby, no naked, frustratingly gorgeous man close by. Just the buzz of campus.

I've sat on this bench for the past hour, and no one has bothered to look at me. Perfect.

What happened last night keeps playing in my head, the sounds, the smells, the image of Darrell's body propped against the wall. And even with all that, the one thing that comes back the most is the look on Michael's face as I ran out of the dorm building this morning. His worry, disappointment, and devastation had been clear.

I'd wanted to get off the moment the bus had

started moving, to just meet him halfway across the parking lot and apologize for leaving. But I couldn't.

Instead, I've sat here thinking about what to do.

I can't go to the police. I knew that before I ran to the bus stop.

What Michael did was wrong, but what Darrell would have done is worse.

He deserved to die.

Michael can't go to jail for that.

A tear falls at the thought, but I quickly wipe it away.

I did nothing.

Well, that's not true.

I'm just as guilty as Michael. Do I want to throw my life away for scum like Darrell? *No.*

Decision made, I head into the large building for my second class. I sat outside, missing the first.

I'll say I'm sick if anyone asks. If I look half as bad as I feel, they'll believe me.

CHAPTER TWENTY-ONE

Michael

The look on my princess's face as she rounds the corner, finding me chatting with her lit professor is more than worth the heart attack I had when she ran earlier.

It's like she really thought I wouldn't track her.

"Hey, princess." I wave her over.

It takes a second for her feet to move, as if her body has forgotten how to do it.

"There's my girl," I greet, dropping a kiss to her cheek, my fingers wrapped around her arm.

I frown at how cold she feels.

Keys weren't the only thing she forgot earlier.

"Lara, Michael said you were unwell. You should have stayed home," Professor Jones admonishes, while I encourage her arms through the sleeves of my jacket. "You go home, and we'll see you in a couple of days."

"No, no," Lara resists.

"Baby, I'm sure Calvin here can advise your other professors. They don't want the other students getting sick, right?" I coerce.

"Anything for our favorite benefactors."

Money talks, even outside of Cromwell Town.

"Michael." It's a plea.

"Come on," I urge. "I want you to meet my other number one girl."

Lara frowns.

The look pleases me. The idea of her being jealous does more than make me happy. Now is not the time to get an erection.

My curious princess forgets all about arguing with me, passing her book bag over for me to shoulder.

"This way." I guide her with our hands entwined. My fingers tingle where we touch, and the feeling spreads up my arm until my heart pounds. A warmth fills my chest, but the pain remains absent.

Shock and bewilderment war it out inside me as we leave the building. Will I ever get used to this?

We're near the parking lot when they come into sight. Daniel and Belle.

My brother always stands out, but with my tiny niece strapped to his chest in a baby sling, it's a sight to behold. One that fixes a part of my heart every time I see it.

"Hi, princess," I coo, stroking Belle's cheek. I

throw Lara a quick look. "Who knows, maybe one day I'll have three princesses, maybe even more," I tease, rubbing her belly.

Lara quickly slaps my hand away from her body. "You will not!" she snaps.

"I wasn't asking," I whisper, dropping a quick kiss to her lips to stop any further response.

The sharp contact with the back of my hand brings old feelings back, but I shove it down quickly. Still, my heart gives a slight flutter of panic.

"Lara, meet Isabelle. Belle, this is your aunt Lara." Just when I think her eyes can't get any rounder, my girl proves me wrong.

Lara reaches out and tickles the baby. Good, it's important for me that Daniel's family and mine get along well. They'll spend a lifetime together.

"Are Mom and Dad still insisting we go to the cabin for some family time tonight?" I ask Daniel, pretending to eat Belle's feet.

Her squeal fills the air, causing her dad and I to smile.

"Yes." My brother shrugs. "Something about families don't yell at each other and Sam being grounded. Mom's upset we all bailed on staying at the cabin for the weekend, too. Do I need to worry about Samantha?"

"No, Kaleb has it handled." The two of us share a look at my words.

He knows too.

"Are my girls going?"

He glares at my question.

"Depends, is mine?" He retaliates, nodding at Lara.

"Point taken." I smirk.

"I got to do a round and then pick up my wife from her class."

"We'll head over now."

I hold my hand out, but Lara ignores it, crossing her arms instead.

"You do security rounds with your daughter strapped to you?"

Daniel nods. "Safest place for her."

"Daniel only checks in on all security desks. He's not actually doing any guarding, not today at least," I reassure her. "Thanks for getting me in the building," I tell Daniel.

He nods, turning to leave.

"Bye, princess," I call out. A squeal and mushed-together words are returned to me as they cross the parking lot, heading toward the back of the building.

Lara turns toward my truck, her arms still folded.

"We'll need to restock the cabin. My family uses it pretty often, but no one had planned to use it after Halloween for a few weeks. Seeing as we have the rest of the day free, we'll do it."

She doesn't respond, but that's okay. I have a lifetime to make her come around.

Plus, angry sex is always good, but after last night, I'm sure any sex with Lara will be great.

CHAPTER TWENTY-TWO

Michael

Putting my truck in park, I turn toward my pouting girl.

"You going to ignore me forever?" I tease.

Her lips twist.

"You got any more princesses?" my sweet girl mumbles.

She's worried I have someone else?

My heart fills that this bothers her, but I like her jealous, not upset.

"No."

When she remains turned toward the door, her head bowed, I grip her knees, turn her enough to pull her legs up. The skirt of her dress slips up, revealing how the pantyhose are stretched and pulled tight between her legs as she spreads wide. I groan at the sight. I pull my own knee onto the truck bench in an effort to get closer.

Hunched over, I brace my left arm on the window behind her, gripping her face with my right hand.

I force her to look at me. "You are my princess."

"And Belle."

"And Belle," I agree with a chuckle. "As are any more baby girls my brother has. Before you, that man was my whole world. That won't change."

Lara looks defeated at my words. She doesn't want to want it.

"I'm yours, but you'll have to learn to share me." Her eyes shoot up at my words, an argument on the tip of her tongue. "Daniel, his family, you, and the babies we will make are my world now. I will die for any of you. Kill for you." I growl against her cheek. "Burn the fucking world for any of you." Pulling back until our noses brush, I swear to her. "No one will love you like I'm about to, Lara Kelsey."

Tears spill out, reaching where my fingers grip her cheeks quickly. Squeezing harder, I pucker her lips, then take them with my own. My tongue is quick to taste her as I explore her mouth.

"You hear me?"

"Yes."

"Yes, sir," I correct.

Lara blinks at me for a second but finally agrees. "Yes, sir."

I dip a finger between us and rub at her covered

clit, just because I can. She hisses as I touch the bruised flesh, her ass lifting off the bench.

"Let's go get some food to feed my family," I say with one final kiss.

"I don't think they have enough food here for you boys," she snarks, looking at the huge grocery store that sits just inside the Cromwell Town border.

Another family investment that panned out.

Her words make me laugh. Being with her lightens my soul, one I long thought to be black through and through.

Her hand warms mine, a feeling I like as we wander down the aisles, picking out items to cook.

"Why do you have a bat in your bedroom?" I ask.

"In case some weirdo broke in." She tuts, but I see the way her mouth tilts up for just a second. "And you mean had? Where is my bat, anyway?"

With Darrell's body.

"What bat? I have no idea what you're talking about," I say aloud, picking up a random jar and pretending to read the label.

Lara releases a breath of disbelief. Shaking her hand, she wiggles my arm. "You owe me a new one."

Placing the jar back, I turn to her. "You won't be needing one. Anyone who breaks into my house has to get through me to get to you, and we'll be at my parents' cabin most weekends." I pause, thinking about how often my family actually stays there. "Half the week, to be honest, but while we're there, you're even safer."

Her steps falter at my words, and the corner of her lip disappears into her mouth.

"This is really fast, Michael." She breathes. "You protected me, and I will always be grateful and won't ever tell," she promises, her words coming in a low whisper. "But this is moving fast, like, really fast." Her eyes flicker nervously up and down the aisle.

Tugging her around to face me, I step closer, leaving very little space between us. Keeping hold of her hand, I raise the other, laying it in the middle of her chest. "Tell me you don't feel this," I challenge.

Lara remains silent, her gaze dropping down.

"Look at me, and tell me," I order.

Her watery eyes snap back up, and her chin quivers as she gives me a small headshake. "I can't." I barely hear her words.

"This thing between us is exactly that, between us. Fuck other people and what they think. I claimed you the minute I saw you. I was just too stubborn to admit it to myself." Pressing a light kiss to the tip of her nose, I add, "You're mine, Lara, just as much as I'm yours."

Lara takes a jittery breath, exhaling a heavy sigh. Blinking quickly, she wets her lips. At the sight of her tongue, I press my mouth to hers.

I feel the way her chest rises and falls quickly beneath my hand. I trail it up her body, loving the way she shivers. Gripping the back of her neck, I hold her still and devour her mouth, only pulling away when I feel her body go languid, the fight leaving her quickly.

Satisfied, I grab the cart again and tug her down the rest of the aisle, her taste on my lips making me want more.

Rounding the corner, we enter another aisle.

"How long are you staying there?" Lara asks, breaking the thick silence between us.

"We," I stress, "should only be there for tonight. Why?"

Lara shrugs.

We've stopped to browse the cereal; Captain Crunch seems to have her attention.

"Add it to the cart, baby."

"No," she answers in a rush.

Letting go of her hand, I move the cart to the side, not wanting to block the aisle. Stepping up behind her, I soothe my hands under my jacket that's far too big on her, and hold her hips. Breathing in her smell, I love how it's mixed with mine, and kiss the back of her neck.

"Princess," I encourage.

"It's nothing, it doesn't matter."

"Everything about you matters to me," I remind her.

Her forefinger traces the letters on the box.

"I wasn't allowed to eat these foods growing up . . . wasn't allowed to eat much, actually."

My heart seizes. Someone like Lara isn't supposed to go hungry.

"My mother married for money. She was terrified Dad would find her ugly and upgrade for a newer, younger wife. Her looks were all she had. But ugly is ugly," she insists, turning her head to me.

"It is," I agree. The thought of a small and hungry Lara makes me homicidal on a level I've never felt before.

"We all have our issues," she whispers to herself. "I stayed skinny by not eating, like I was taught to, but after I moved out, I researched and educated myself on health and fitness. I eat in moderation now, most of the time," she admits shakily. "But I have a deal with myself," she whispers like it's a secret. "I get to eat whatever I want for breakfast on weekends as long as . . ."

"Seven miles every day, no excuses," I finish for her.

"You really were watching."

"Protecting," I correct, with a playful nip at her neck.

Lara sighs. "When I moved away to college, I picked one close to home in California, but when I heard about Hampstock College opening and how they were offering huge discounts for students willing to transfer in, well, I couldn't wait to get farther away." She turns to face me fully, her eyes pleading. "Does that make me a bad daughter?"

My hands frame her face. "No, baby." I shake my head. "That makes you human." I bring her mouth to mine, kissing her like it can fix the damage her mother did.

Fuck, I love her.

Although I had been happy for Daniel, a part of me never really understood how he fell for Charlie so completely with just one look. Now I do.

I meant every word in that truck. God help anyone who tries to take her from me.

Lara moans into my mouth, earning us a scandalized look from a passing woman.

"Are you sore?" I ask, already knowing the answer. "I need you, come on. We're leaving, and Captain is coming with us. We'll work off the calories another way."

I reach over her shoulder, grabbing a box.

"It'll go to waste."

"How? You can take the rest to your dorm, or they can stay at mine for when we're there."

Yeah, baby, there's no escaping now.

Her cheeks flush. She can deny it all she wants, but her body will always be truthful.

No one had better be in that cabin when we get there. I'm not waiting until tonight to get my girl alone.

"Daddy, look."

A child's voice grabs my attention, but I don't know why. Instinct maybe. I turn to see a small girl, around five or six, pointing at something out of view. A large man stands beside her, pushing their cart. He glances into the aisle.

That saying it takes one to know one is one hundred percent true. My eyes roll over the man in our aisle, assessing and deliberate.

His gaze turns to me. It's empty, void.

My whole body reacts. The hair on the back of my neck stands up, and my muscles vibrate with energy.

His baseball cap sits low, making it hard to see his face, but he's around my age, maybe a little older. He nods in my direction.

He knows.

His left hand reaches out to rest on the top of his daughter's head.

A message.

His daughter is off-limits to killers like us.

His face morphs into a smile, his whole face transforming as he lovingly looks down at her. The child grins up at him, giggling as he tickles her chin with the end of her braid.

Catching his gaze again, I nod. Reaching out, I wrap Lara's braid around my hand, using it to pull her close. A message returned.

His family is safe if my family is safe.

"Let's go, princess."

Head tilted back in my tight grip, she finds my eyes for a second before I look away, needing to keep him in sight. "Can we get your mom some flowers?"

"Baby, if you can get it within two minutes, you can have anything you want."

"There's a joke about you somewhere in there."
My cheeky girl grins.

"Your ass is going to pay for that later," I warn
her, releasing her braid.

I steer her to the other end of the aisle, not
wanting to get too close.

Time for us to leave.

Lara snags a pretty bunch of flowers on our way
to check out. We're in the queue for ten minutes, and
it's ten minutes too long. I can feel my skin crawling.
The idea of another killer being this close to my girl
tests every bit of my control.

My eyes track him as he checks out a few tills
down. His eyes are glued to his daughter, and it helps
ease me slightly. He wants to keep her safe, so he
wouldn't risk anything with her here.

I wouldn't hurt a child, but he doesn't know that.
The same way I can't know that he wouldn't try to
hurt Lara.

"You okay?" Lara asks.

"Of course. I'm sorry, princess. I'm just tired. We
didn't sleep much last night." It was both the right
and wrong thing to say.

Lara's smile drops, her throat bobbing. She pulls
away from me emotionally, but at least now she's just
as eager to leave as I am.

My head turns from left to right, taking everyone
in as we leave, descending the steps quickly.

A commotion to my left draws everyone's attention. I immediately step around Lara, putting myself between the two.

The man I spotted in the store rushes over to his little girl, who is on the floor crying. A woman kneels in front of her, wiping away her tears. By the time he reaches them, the tears have stopped and been replaced by a smile.

Keeping a sound grip on Lara's hand, I keep us moving. Adrenaline courses through me. My girl remains completely oblivious.

Thankfully.

The woman in front of the girl tilts her head up with a bright smile ready for a killer.

Lulu!

I recognize her. She's Samantha's friend, they went to school together.

The man crouches, joining the two girls.

Lulu's stepdad interrupts the conversation, his hand violent as it rips her away from the small family.

My feet stop.

"Michael?" Lara questions, confused.

She searches the parking lot, just as I had. Maybe she was paying attention. "I'm scared."

My head snaps to her, and my left hand tilts her head back. "You never have to be afraid with me. Anyone who wants to get to you will have to go through me first."

Watery eyes peer up at me. "You'll protect me?"

"Until my last breath," I swear.

I kiss her forehead, sealing the promise.

Satisfied, she lets me lead her to my truck.

I glance back at the steps once she's safely tucked away inside, the groceries on the bench beside her.

He's still standing there, the girl now on his hip.

Our eyes meet as I return the cart. He turns to look at where Lulu sits crying in the back of a beat-up Ford.

His eyes find me again. It takes me a second to realize . . . he's asking for permission.

I frown. Lulu is a good girl, stuck in a situation my brothers and I meant to take care of two years ago.

He looks at the car again, but it's not Lulu that he glares at. It's the two in the front.

He wants her parents.

That I can oblige.

I give a discreet nod but then give a quick shake of my head, my gaze zeroing in on Lulu.

Them he can have, her he can't.

A smile spreads across his face.

And with that, we go our separate ways.

My phone is out before I'm even in the truck. My family needs to get to the cabin quicker than tonight.

There's a killer in town, one that doesn't carry the Cromwell name.

He should be busy enough with those two, but who knows when he'll strike. When it comes to family, you can never be too safe.

And there's power in numbers.

Our lucky number is three.

Daniel, Kaleb, and I.

CHAPTER TWENTY-THREE

Michael

My body is vibrating; there's no other way to describe it. I'm wound up and ready to blow.

We're in the truck on the way to my parents, so killing someone just isn't an option.

It's barely one in the afternoon, and my family has dropped all their plans, including work, to come out to our cabin. They were willing to squirrel away here just because I asked them to.

That's the meaning of family. Blind faith, no questions asked.

Lara sits beside me in my truck, being her perfect self. No longer scared, she's happy for me to take control.

I glance over at her. "Do you need to call in to

work? I didn't see your schedule on your laptop or in your dorm."

Lara squints at me. "No, I got fired, but now that you mention it, you shouldn't go through my laptop . . . it's rude."

"Why?" I ask. "What are you hiding?"

"Nothing," she insists defensively.

I look at her quickly. "Porn?"

She rolls her eyes before looking out the passenger window. "Never mind, look all you want. There's nothing to find."

That's better.

Grinning, I reach over the groceries to lay my hand on her thigh. Her pantyhose feels soft beneath my palm. I give a gentle squeeze. "Why did you get fired?"

Lara shrugs, heaving a deep sigh. "The owner is a sleazebag. He wanted sex, I find him repulsive, the rest is history," she says like it's nothing.

The truck jolts slightly.

"He fired you because you wouldn't fuck him?" I seethe.

Turning away from the passenger window, Lara faces me with a frown. "It's not a big deal. I'm not the first."

"Lowe's restaurant in town, right?"

Lara nods.

"I'll take care of it."

"Michael—" She starts, but I cut her off.

"I'll take care of it," I repeat.

And I'm not waiting until next Halloween. Mother-fucker picked the wrong woman.

Lara's hand lands on mine, in thanks or to calm me, I don't know, but either way, I let her warmth encasing my hand sink in.

No panic, no pain. *This woman really is something else.*

"Think your mom will like the flowers?" she asks, changing the subject.

I glance at her briefly, not wanting to take my eyes off Ellis Road for too long. Truckers and people passing through use this road to make up time or to avoid a traffic control issue, so they dip off the I-90 and join back on a few towns over.

Great for Duke and other businesses in town but not so good for community safety. They drive like Kaleb . . . a fucking menace.

Turning onto my family's land, I drive past the damaged tree on the edge of the property. *He's not the only menace.*

"She'll love them. What mother doesn't love one of her babies getting her flowers?" I wink.

"Not funny." Lara frowns.

"I'm not teasing. That woman is going to enjoy having another daughter."

She likes the idea. Lara's eyes are pleading as they search my face for an ounce of a lie. Finding none, my girl smiles.

"I've only met her once! This is the first time I'll

be meeting her as your . . ." She stumbles, unsure what to call us.

Something that needs clearing up now.

"My wife."

I hold up my finger when she opens her mouth to argue.

"My wife," I repeat. "Say it."

My stubborn princess shakes her head. "We're not married."

Yet.

"You're right." I nod, waiting for her to relax before informing her, "We'll go to the courthouse tomorrow."

Breath huffs out of her in disbelief, her mouth open, ready to argue, but she's so caught off guard, she has no words.

I'm possessive and unreasonable when it comes to her, but it's for a good reason. Reaching over, I cup her cheek. "You're my life now, Lara, and you'll be my wife."

She gives me the same pleading look as earlier. The one that tells me she wants it but won't admit it. Her big brown eyes peer at me, her pupils dilated with desire. Her mouth says one thing, and her eyes say another. Her chest expands on a heavy sigh, a blush spreading up her neck quickly.

Her gaze drops to my mouth.

Fuck it, we're not making it back to the cabin.

Pulling the truck to the side of the private road, I

eye the time. Hopefully, my family won't drop everything too quickly.

"Come here, princess." I gesture to my lap.

Her face flushes, seeing my hands fumble with my belt buckle.

"Michael, no."

But her words lack conviction.

Twisting in her seat, Lara looks out the cab window, back from where we came.

"Your whole family is coming here."

I nod, pulling my already hard cock out.

"They could see us," she hisses.

"Then you'd better stop wasting time. Lose the jacket and climb over here."

Her plump bottom lip is tortured by her teeth while she decides what to do.

"Lara," I stress.

Giving in to the inevitable, she shrugs out of my jacket, leaving it bunched by the door. She climbs around the grocery bag and settles onto my jean-clad knee, using the wheel and the dash to steady herself as she moves.

When she stills, I move her until she faces the front of the truck, her legs together with mine caging them in, giving me better leverage with spread legs.

"Mind your head," I warn, lowering the visor. I want to see her face while we fuck.

One hand works my cock as the other lifts her dress. Her pantyhose is thick and made of wool to keep her warm, but they rip quickly when my hands pull from the middle out. The pale skin of her round ass is a stark contrast to the black pantyhose that frames it.

My fingers run along the ripped seam, tearing them further until her pussy is bared.

"Are you wet?" I ask, but she doesn't need to speak. My fingers are already probing her mound, finding her wet and ready.

"You say no, but your body says yes. Does the idea of my family catching us with my dick in you excite you, princess?"

I smack her ass when she doesn't answer.

"Yes," she admits shamefully.

"Me too," I confess, kissing her cheek. "Hands on the steering wheel, Lara. They don't move."

"Yes, sir."

Gripping her hips tightly, I slowly lower her onto my cock, savoring the feel of her tight heat.

Lara hisses, resisting when I try to sink the rest of the way in.

I'm large and thick, so biting the bullet, I make quick work of burying the other half of my erection.

"Ahh, ahh," Lara cries out with every thrust.

Gripping her ass cheek, I squeeze, flexing my hips again.

"Please, stop."

I freeze at her words.

"It hurts."

"Good." I tap her ass. "You're dripping."

"It's different, not like last night."

Fuck, the pounding I gave her last night might just screw me over today.

"Shit." I curse, dropping my forehead to her clothed back. "Lift," I guide, removing myself from her body.

My wet cock meets the cold air, making me hiss. It bobs between my legs, desperate to get back to her warmth.

Lara starts to slide off my lap.

Wrapping her braid around my hand, I still her. "Stay, your pussy isn't the only option."

"No! That hurt last night." She panics.

"It's either your pussy or ass. Choice is yours."

I wait impatiently.

"I really am too sore."

Our eyes meet in the mirror.

I nod. "Say it," I encourage.

Lara shakes her head.

I give her braid another pull. "You can either say it, and I lubricate my cock, or you don't, and you'd better hope your juices are enough to ease my way inside."

Her eyes dilate.

Well, shit.

"Fuck my ass."

Shame, I guess a raw ass fucking will have to wait for another day.

I don't stay disappointed for long.

Keeping our gaze locked, I blindly rummage in the grocery bag. Frustrated, I tip the brown bag over, contents spilling out onto the bench. My target rolls free.

Grabbing the glass bottle, I lift it to my teeth, bite the cap, and twist. The lid shoots across the cab, pinging onto the dash as I spit it out, not caring where it goes.

"Lift and hold your dress."

Her hands grapple with the material, and the steering wheel holds her up as she hunches over it.

Quickly, I pour a good amount of olive oil into my hand, palming it onto my thick, heavy cock. The wetter, the better. Happy with the coating, my slippery fingers seek out her asshole.

She'd been an anal virgin last night, but she took a small portion, just enough to coat her insides with my cum.

Today, she's taking all nine inches of me, balls deep.

Her body resists my digit but a firm push eases it in.

Lara tries to shift forward more away from my exploring fingers, but with the steering wheel pressed against her, she has nowhere to go. My coated hand grabs her ass cheek, blunt nails biting as she's spread wide.

"Michael," she complains, embarrassed.

"I'm about to watch my cock sink into your ass. It hardly matters if I watch as I finger fuck it first."

A second finger joins.

Lara glances back at me. Her plump bottom lip

sits between her teeth. Her hips wiggle, pain and fullness etched on her face.

She's as ready as she can be.

Bringing her back down to my lap, I run my hands over the top of her thighs, waiting until I feel her body relax.

This is about to be intense and painful enough. Tense muscles will just make her resist me more.

"Hold your dress higher."

I help gather it, passing it off to her left hand.

"The other on the wheel," I remind her. My palm on her back pushes her forward, creating a vee between our bodies.

The perfect view for what's about to happen.

I shift my feet closer in, bringing her legs tighter together while my hands lift and spread her ass cheeks.

My cock doesn't need me to guide it. It's like a heat-seeking missile ready to go off. The broad head nudges at her freshly used hole. The clench it has on my tip is out of this world.

Lara whimpers.

My eyes stay glued to where my cock invades her body. Her ring turns white as it struggles to swallow me.

I'm barely inside, and Lara is crying. She's not used to it, but a few more times, and her body will crave it as much as I do.

Anal is my go-to. It's perfect when you can't have

your partner touching you, although fucking in my truck is a first for me.

"Ahh," she cries out as several inches of my dick disappear into her.

I wedge my hand between her legs, seeking out her slit. Coating my finger, I search for her sensitive nub. Rubbing harshly, I try to push her higher.

"Shhh, baby. You can take it. You're doing so good. I wish you could see how well your ass swallows me."

Her pussy weeps at my words.

"It hurts." She sniffles.

"I know." I kiss her back.

Attacking her button more, I have her shaking and on edge within seconds. The minute she falls over the edge into a blissful orgasm, my hands pull her down, embedding myself fully.

Her scream is pain-filled, but a fresh wave of orgasm rolls over her. Her empty pussy clenches, the ripples tickling at the underside of my shaft. Her asshole squeezes me painfully.

Sobs roll out of her from where she's dropped against the wheel.

"I can't, I can't," she wails.

"You can, Lara," I pant.

My control is on its last thread, and I'm seconds away from pounding her ass. Throwing my head back, I clench my teeth, waiting for her pain to decrease.

The shake of the sobs wracking her body makes my cock twitch and leak in her ass.

Wait, wait, wait, I remind myself. Forcing out a long breath, I'm praying not to blow my load.

The sound of an engine is enough to cool my blood.

A glance in the rearview mirror shows my dad's SUV approaching quickly.

Fuck my life.

"Princess, we have company," I point out. "No, no," I rush when Lara tries to jump away.

We both cry out as she drops back onto me.

"We don't have time. Lean back into me," I insist, rearranging the skirt of her dress. The flowy material is enough to cover my lap and conceal our attachment.

I'm still panting and Lara crying when my parents' car pulls up beside my truck. Thank fuck mine stands slightly higher making our situation more discreet.

I roll down the window, giving a small wave.

"You guys okay?" My dad frowns.

I nod, unable to speak. Lara's asshole took on a whole new level of tightness the minute their car stopped. Her essence flows out onto my lap.

She's excited.

One of these days, I'm going to have to take her out near the interstate and fuck her in the bed of my truck as people pass. Close enough she can see them, but they can't see her.

"Your truck giving you trouble?" Mom asks, leaning around my dad to see us.

"I don't think it's the car having trouble," Dad snarks.

He's where Kaleb gets his smart mouth from, I think with a roll of my eyes.

Mom finally spots Lara's red and wet face. "Oh, baby." She coos, "Whatever he did, he's sorry." Helen looks at me as if to say, *right?*

"Why did you assume I did something?" I huff.

Lara turns, giving me a glare over her shoulder.

"Do you want to hop in this car and come with us?"

Over my dead body.

"We're going to the same place, Mom," I point out, my irritation obvious.

Lara swipes at her cheeks, pointlessly brushing the tears away since new ones replace them quickly.

"I'm okay, I promise." Lara sniffles.

"We're working it out," I add when my parents hesitate to leave.

"Okay," Dad finally agrees, "your sister is already here. Kaleb fetched her."

That was quick. We came straight here from the store. They must have already been together.

"We'll just finish working this out and be down soon."

We all give an awkward wave, but they finally leave.

"Wait for them to get far enough that they can't

see, and then back to how you were." My words are choppy, my movements desperate as my hand moves back between her legs. I need her to enjoy this too.

Lara is panting and moaning by the time the car is almost out of sight.

I can't wait any longer. How slow are they fucking driving? It'll have to be good enough.

Slowly, I pry her off my lap. My cock withdraws, then I bring her back down, slowly at first.

Up and down. Our actions repeat over and over until the windows are fogged, and the cab fills with nothing but pants, moans, and soft sobs.

"What are you?" I ask, bringing her back to our earlier conversation.

So lost in the feel of my cock, she doesn't answer.

"What are you?" I ask again, demanding an answer with a particularly brutal shove of my hips.

Still, moans and whimpers are the only things to leave her mouth.

Sliding my hand to the small of her back, I push her forward, forcing her upper body to lie flat on the wheel. It lifts her off me to the point that only my tip is engulfed. With all the power I can, I lift my ass off the bench seat and force three quick thrusts of my cock into her ass.

Her scream builds my pleasure.

"What are you?" I growl, yanking her down to the bench with me, bottoming out inside her as we sit back down.

"Your wife," she screams, her asshole gripping me

to a point beyond tortured pleasure. My cock can't take much more of this.

But I need more. More pain, more pleasure, more Lara.

I'm beyond thinking, my mind blank as I rip my sweater over my head. Animalistic as I tear the top of her dress right down the back. All the time fucking her hard and fast.

Lara helps me push the body of her dress down, the ripped material bunching at her slim waist.

My hands grope her breasts. Our skin thuds when her back connects with my chest.

"Lick," I demand, bringing my fingers to her mouth.

She does without question. Sucking two digits in, she swirls them with her tongue.

The change in angle does something for her, even more so than before. Her body starts to move above me.

Our movements are manic, frantic, and wild.

Friction builds between us in all ways.

I need more oil. The bottle is slippery on the wet seat and over half empty since most of it spilled out. I managed to get it between us and just pour the rest over my crotch not willing to move her too far away from my body to do it properly.

It's enough.

I fuck her harder than I have before, which after last night, is a feat.

The truck moves with the power of our lovemaking.

I build higher and higher.

Lara's head falls back against my shoulder, and it's enough to set me off. With a roar, I come harder than I ever have before. An explosion happens inside her—streams and streams of cum flow out of me.

This woman was made for me.

So lost in the longest orgasm of my life, I don't notice the truck pull up behind us nor do I hear the boots approaching.

I'm startled when my door is ripped open.

Daniel appears, his face consumed with worry.

Knowing there's no danger, I don't stop my movements, willing my pleasure to keep flowing.

Lara rushes to cover herself, but my hands are plastered to her breasts, and I'm not willing to let her go.

"You okay?" Daniel huffs.

I nod, still pumping my essence into my girl.

The door slams closed just as my stream stops. Lara buries her head into her hands.

"Your brother just caught us." Her words are muffled.

"Another thing you'll get used to. He and Charlie go at it like bunnies," I joke.

"What's the other thing I'll get used to?" she asks, letting me pull her back into my chest.

"My dick in your ass." My fingers seek out her clit.

"Don't think I didn't notice you didn't come with me."

"It's okay," she whispers, her small hand on my forearm.

But it's not okay. Her body had been right there with me on the peak of pleasure. I'm nothing if not fair.

My body ignites again at her touch, my dick hardening. My breath catches.

The passenger door opens, and my brother's large body appears as I help my girl rub out another orgasm.

He throws a gym bag onto the bench seat. The plastic wrapping of the forgotten food crinkles under the weight of the bag. "Charlie's. They should fit her."

Lara is too lost in pleasure to care that he's here, or maybe she hasn't noticed. I tease her nipple with my other hand.

"You need any clothes?" he asks me.

No. I have my own gym bag.

But what actually comes out is a long-drawn-out moan. I shake my head.

Daniel nods, closing the door again.

The jolt of the truck, the feel of her back on my chest, the slight burn I feel in my skin, the pressure of her pleasure bearing down on my tool. It's just too much.

My still hard cock twitches inside her, and my eyes widen.

I'm coming again.

This time, I take Lara with me, both of us drowning as my brother's truck passes. His hand is stretched out, covering his wife's eyes.

Laughing, I clutch my girl.

I've said it before, and I'll say it again.

This woman owns me.

With a final thrust, I finish filling her with a piece of myself.

CHAPTER TWENTY-FOUR

Lara

I try not to waddle as I walk into the cabin.

The word cabin does not do this house justice. Being in the dark last time and then caught up in everything the next day, I never stopped to take in the house and land.

It's beautiful.

Lush trees of all colors frame the road on either side, the forest running long and deep. The wooden house sits on the edge of Cromwell Lake, a dock not too far away.

The kind of vacation home people dream of.

The inside is cozy and homey. Large chairs covered in blankets fill the living space. An image of Michael and me snuggled under the red blanket on the chair by the fire makes me smile.

"We'd do more than snuggle." Michael winks, touching the red blanket as we pass.

"Michael!" I hiss, looking around to see if anyone heard.

"You have my cum dripping out of your ass, and you're shy because I want to fuck you in front of a log fire? You're adorable." He laughs, pulling me close and kissing the side of my head.

I move away, unsure how he feels about me being so close.

The truck had been . . . something else. But he may not want to be touched when we're not in the throes of passion.

"There you two are." Kaleb smiles. "Thought I would have to come tow your truck down here."

Michael flips his brother off. "My truck works just fine." He grins.

Kaleb points at Michael, the knife in his hand gleaming under the incandescent lights. "I knew it!" He shakes his head.

Oh God.

A sound of embarrassment leaves me. Raising my hands, I cover my face, mortified. Kaleb chuckles, but I feel Michael step forward, the heat of him calming my body. It never fails to react to him.

At the light brush of his lips on the tip of my nose, I squint at him through a gap in my fingers.

"We've done nothing wrong," Michael reassures me.

My mind wonders at his words. *Haven't we?*

His face darkens. "We've done nothing wrong," he insists, his tone demanding that I believe him . . . so I do.

What happened needs to stay in the past. I can't let it ruin whatever this is, what it could be. Michael was protecting me. That's all that matters.

I take Michael's outstretched hand but step back to leave a gap between our bodies.

Looking at the space between us, he smiles, releasing my hand. His fingers are confident as they slide along the small of my back and onto my hip. His grip is forceful, bringing me closer until I'm glued to his side.

His thumb brushes back and forth on the sliver of skin where Charlie's borrowed top doesn't quite reach the band of the black leggings. My body responds instantly.

Will I ever not want this man?

Kaleb and a petite brunette stand at the kitchen island chopping tomatoes. She's beautiful, her smile bright, and her eyes shine as the two laugh together.

"Who brought food?" Michael asks, gesturing to the mostly prepped food spread over the countertop.

No one answers verbally, but Kaleb waves his knife slightly.

"Thanks." Michael smiles, not mentioning the food we picked up. That's probably best since most of it is rolling around the floorboard of his truck. They don't want to eat that.

My face heats at how it got there.

His large hand pats my ass. Is he thinking the same thing?

Worth the loss. I grin, flicking my eyes to his face and looking away quickly.

How had I only met this man a few days ago? My chest fills with something I don't want to acknowledge. It's not normal. What I saw him do wasn't normal, yet my grin doesn't slip as I peek at him again.

"Well, that's better. I'll take a smile over tears any day," Christopher cheers, raising his drink as he joins us in the kitchen, his wife, Daniel and baby Belle, who is still strapped to her daddy's chest, follow close.

"We'd like you to join us at the county clerk's office tomorrow," Michael announces as if this isn't a surprise to me either.

Everyone freezes, including me.

"I've asked Judge Greene to meet us there and marry us. He's agreed. I put a call into Molly. She wants us there a few hours beforehand to fill out and file the paperwork so she can sort the marriage license while the judge performs the wedding."

Upside of small towns is people make things happen, I guess.

"There's a park across the street. It's pretty," he reassures me, like that's the problem.

I try to shy away from everyone's eyes, but Michael won't let me. His hold stays tight.

The whole room just stares at us, their eyes moving between Michael and me.

Helen screams, rushing forward to envelop me in a hug so tight I practically feel my bones shift.

"Congratulations, baby," she whispers to Michael over my shoulder.

One by one, I'm passed around the group, each welcoming me to the family.

No one hugs Michael, not until Daniel approaches him.

Passing Belle off to the woman who I assume is her mother, Daniel grips hold of Michael's neck. The two lock eyes silently.

The loud, boisterous noise of the kitchen fades as I watch the two connect.

After a few minutes, the larger man pulls his younger brother in, hugging him like his life depends on it. By the time they separate, I'm not the only one in tears.

"You get used to it," the small brunette whispers. "Their bond," she clarifies. "Charlie." She offers her hand.

"Charlotte," Daniel corrects in his growly voice.

Charlie rolls her eyes. "My husband is the only one who really calls me that."

"Lara." I smile, shaking her hand.

"How's the foot?" Helen asks, joining us.

"Oh, perfect. Stopped hurting a few days after I left here," I say, wiggling it to show I'm as good as new.

"You're perfect," she praises, framing my face.

Tears fill my eyes. Why couldn't my own mother be like her?

"What happened to your foot?" Charlie frowns, handing Belle off to her insistent grandmother. According to Helen's grin, this is exactly what she had planned when she came here.

"Samantha," Michael tuts. "Speaking of, where is she?"

"Upstairs," Helen says quietly. "She and your father argued about her grounding, and Kaleb ended up taking her upstairs for a talking-to."

"She was being a brat, so she gets a time-out," Kaleb calls over, picking the knife back up. "Let's eat, shall we? Celebrate my brother getting married."

"You're next." Christopher laughs, pointing his beer bottle at Kaleb.

"Fuck, no," he protests.

But I see the way his mouth lifts slightly.

Belle draws my attention, squealing and babbling to her Uncle Michael. Stepping closer, I sigh as the heat of his hand sears my ass. My body really does crave this man like nothing else. Michael reaches out to take Belle, kissing her cheek as he brings her to his chest. Seeing how gentle and loving he is, I know I won't be able to fight him and his demands for a future for much longer.

The murder that happened last night is one problem. My heart is another.

CHAPTER TWENTY-FIVE

Michael

Sam finally came downstairs, willing to mingle with the family just in time to join us for dinner. Her mood lifted immediately after finding out about my engagement.

Seems my sister is happy I'm taken, or rather, that Lara is taken.

A thought I'm not diving into.

My whole family has been great and beyond supportive. Not that I expected anything less since they'd been the same with Daniel.

I stand propped against the doorframe of the kitchen, watching Charlie and my girl help my mom clean up the dinner mess, unable and unwilling to let Lara out of my sight.

"He's a good man," Charlie whispers, her words only just reaching me.

Lara peeks over at me.

"You won't find anyone as loyal. Once he loves someone, that's it. He's never letting go."

What am I, a fucking retriever?

"The brothers have that in common, that and a few other things. If you ever need to talk, I'm here."

Lara frowns at her words, not understanding but I do. I give Charlie a look that she needs to behave. She knows better.

My girl knows I'm a killer. She doesn't need to know the rest. Not before she's fully bound to me, at least.

Daniel joins me in the doorway. "Go control your wife," I mutter.

"She'd only enjoy it."

I turn to him, my mouth open slightly.

Two years later and it still shakes me to my core when my big brother makes a joke.

"And stop bringing my wife fries and milkshakes," he growls, kicking away from the door. That's more like it.

"She likes them!" I protest.

"I know, that's why I buy them." He glares. Leaning down, he molds his mouth to Charlie's, peppering tiny kisses to her lips. Belle reaches for her mother's hair. Strapped to her dad, she's more than happy to have her mom and dad close.

Lara blushes, watching as the couple kisses next to

her at the counter. Her hip is propped against the counter, drawing my eyes to where the blue sports top ends on her midriff.

We really need to buy her outfits for when we stay here. Her clothes and the rest of her things will be at my house soon, but I prefer to keep my room here stocked since we come often enough. Maybe a shopping trip and a new wardrobe will help ease the fact that I'm about to upheave her whole world. If nothing else, it'll be a chance for the ladies to bond.

Mom leaves the kitchen, busy collecting more dirty dishes, leaving the four of us alone, so I take my chance.

"You really do like to watch," I tease my girl as I sneak up behind her, my chin resting softly on her shoulder.

She shivers when my lips brush her ear, my teeth tugging at her lobe.

"Do not!" she insists.

"Are you wet?"

"Michael!" she shrieks, horrified. Spinning around, she dislodges me.

"Michael Cromwell, you stop annoying my new daughter," Mom shouts from the other room.

Lara's breath catches.

"Told you." I wink.

"Mom, Daniel won't let me hold the baby," I whine, reaching for Belle.

"Make your own," Daniel replies, slapping my hands away.

"I'm working on it," I answer smugly.

"Then you'd better learn to put your dick in a different hole."

I choke at his words.

"Daniel!" Charlie reprimands.

But I'm in too much shock to say anything.

That's the funniest and the filthiest joke he's ever made!

Lara's face takes on a shade of red yet to be named.

"Ignore him." Charlie rubs Lara's arm. "I do."

At his wife's words, Daniel finally passes me the baby. "Is that a fact?" he quizzes.

His hands engulf Charlie's waist, pulling her into his body. Will I ever be able to do that with Lara? Hold her close without having to give myself a pep talk first. To be able to reach out and not worry about possibly feeling pain and panic?

The memory of her back touching my bare chest in the truck and the thrill it caused rushes over me. I'm touching Lara more than I've ever touched anyone.

Will it ever be instinctively and without thought? *Maybe one day.*

Sam skips into the room, stealing Belle while I'm distracted.

"I'm her favorite. She loves me more," my sister gloats.

"Not true!" I huff. "Charlie, Sam's being mean." My sister-in-law gives me an indulgent smile while her husband sucks at her neck. "Give me another niece so we can both hold one," I demand. I take Belle back, holding her close. It's amazing how healing she's been for my brother and me.

"I'm working on it," Daniel tells me with a glare, his hands dropping to his wife's ass.

Get a room.

A second later, they do just that. Daniel eagerly pulls his wife from the room, heading for the stairs.

"Belle," Charlie protests.

"I got her," I call out.

"Where are they going?" Dad asks, entering just as the couple sneaks out.

"Bed. They're pretty tired. Charlie was practically falling asleep on her feet," I lie.

Mom tuts, joining us again. "We should help more. They're overwhelmed."

I try not to smile. The opposite is true.

"We'll take her all night. I miss having a baby wake me at two a.m.," she jokes. "You kids go play somewhere and stop hogging my grandbaby."

Play? The woman forgets how old we are.

"Movie?" Kaleb asks.

"Not scary!" Sam insists.

CHAPTER TWENTY-SIX

Lara

Tonight was fun. I never expected to love his family, let alone this much, this fast.

I really did miss out as a child.

The resentment I've always felt toward my parents grows as we step onto the top floor. It didn't have to be this way; I didn't have to be this way.

No one is perfect, but my parents hadn't been ready for a child, and neither am I, which is why I made my appointment for tomorrow. Luckily, I'd had loose change in my bag for the pay phone at the school earlier. Now, I just need enough time to sneak away to attend it.

Michael leaves me at the door of his bedroom. Patiently, I wait as he hurries next door, carrying a tray full of food and refreshments to the room farther down.

He doesn't turn on the light. Instead, he slips inside the dark room with only the light from the hall to guide him.

Helen creeps up the stairs behind me.

"Hi," I whisper, turning around.

"Everything okay?" she asks.

I shrug, unsure. When large hands settle on my waist just under my breasts, I realize she wasn't asking me.

"They're fast asleep," Michael replies, keeping his voice low.

Helen worries her lip.

"Mom, they're okay. Just tired."

Helen nods. "I'll offer to take Belle next weekend. Give them some time to relax."

Even I can see she feels mom guilt at the idea of the couple being so worn out they went to bed early.

She's a good mom.

Guilt swirls in my own tummy at not telling her the real reason they went to bed.

Michael presses a kiss to the back of my head.

"They'll be okay. Besides, we need to save up all the babysitting for when they have baby number two," he teases.

Helen grins at the idea, her whole face lighting up. "Very true," she agrees. "Well, I'll leave you two to get some sleep."

I blush even though her words hold no innuendo.

"Good night," Michael and I echo.

As I cross the threshold, the room feels smaller than a few days ago. My heart tries to escape my chest when he joins me in the bedroom.

My breaths grows labored, and the man hasn't even touched me.

"You're still sore," he tells me, but I nod anyway. "So how about we put that sweet mouth of yours to good use?" he leers, knocking the door closed with his foot.

CHAPTER TWENTY-SEVEN

Lara

Michael's foot nudges mine under the kitchen table for the second time. Again, I ignore him.

My cheeks burn, the memories of last night still fresh.

After a third nudge, I finally give in.

Raising a brow, I silently ask, "What?"

"Nothing," he says, his eyes dropping to my mouth.

I bite my lip, ducking my gaze away.

"Michael Cromwell, you stop embarrassing that girl," Helen berates him.

"What did I do?" he demands.

Helen narrows her eyes at her son. "I don't know, but I'm sure it was something."

I giggle.

Helen presses a kiss to my hair as she leaves the kitchen, adding, "Give me a shout if he gives you any trouble."

"Yes, ma'am." I play along.

"Seems Sam's been replaced as my mom's favorite." Michael winks.

"Nuh-uh, take that back!" Sam demands from farther up the table.

"Just calling it as I see it."

Leaning back, I soak in the sibling playfulness.

I'm definitely having more than one child. One day.

I don't want to spoil the mood, but I need to tell Michael about going into town today . . . alone.

Taking a swig of orange juice, I dive in headfirst. "Charlie, can I catch a ride with you when you go to college later? I need to go to my dorm."

"Umm . . ." Charlie stalls, looking at Michael.

Michael's fork pauses halfway to his mouth. "What do you need to go home for?"

I prepared for this. "I need to go into town to run some errands," I say, trying to stay casual and calm.

"We're going into town later to meet Molly at the clerk's office," he reminds me.

Shit. I was hoping he'd forget about that.

"No, it's okay. I need to go home first."

The cutlery clanks on his plate as he lays it down, elbows propped on the table, and his fingers intertwined under his chin. I have his full attention.

"Why?"

"To change," I say like it's obvious, gesturing at

208

another set of Charlie's borrowed clothes I have on. The hoodie is nice and thin, but the leggings barely fit.

I take another drink of orange juice.

"Try that again," he suggests, not buying it.

The conversation around us continues to flow, leaving us in a bubble of our own. Who knew you could feel so alone at a table full of people? A sigh stutters out of me.

"Open that mouth and lie, see what happens," he dares.

Fuck.

I twirl my glass, the liquid sloshing dangerously close to the top. Michael's hand grips the glass, stilling my movements.

"I need to go for a run."

His head goes back, confusion washing over his face.

"Okay. You could have just said that." He pauses, seeming to think for a second. "How's your ankle?"

"Good." I nod.

"We'll go for a run, meet Molly, and then we can run your errands before we meet my family at the county clerk's office."

"No," I rush out.

Michael lifts a brow. "We're getting married, Lara."

"I need to do the errands alone."

Subtle, real subtle.

His brows shoot up when he realizes it's not the marriage I'm protesting.

My heart flutters at the thought of marrying this man. I know I should be kicking and screaming, and if we were somewhere else, I might. But here and now, with this loving and loyal family, I just can't get myself to say the words.

I barely know Michael, but I've never felt this way before. Besides, something tells me fighting this would get me nowhere.

My mind reminds me of the last two times that Michael has punished me—in my dorm when I said someone else's name and in the truck when I wouldn't repeat what he wanted. Both times had been . . . painful and erotic.

My panties dampen. Maybe arguing wouldn't be so bad.

"No."

"No?"

"You heard me," he says calmly, picking his fork back up.

And just like that, the conversation is over.

Muffled shouting interrupts our morning. All three men stand at once.

"The fuck is that?" Kaleb asks.

Michael shrugs. "Dad's just gone to the door. Give him a second."

Turning in my seat, I try to get a look outside but can only see as far as the living room.

"Where's Mom?" Daniel asks, his concern clear.

Michael leans to the left, getting a better look into the other room. "By the front door. Which means Dad's outside."

"Take the baby upstairs and stay there with her," Daniel orders Charlie. His voice is growly and rough like the last few times I've heard it. But this time, it's also sharp and forceful.

Charlie pales, her eyes dashing to the front door. The man is a human mountain, but as he cradles his wife's face to run his nose against hers, you'd think he was nothing more than a marshmallow. Definitely not the same man who cleaned my crime scene of a bedroom to within an inch of its life and disposed of a dead body.

I melt.

"Go with her," Michael tells me, getting my attention with a tug of my hair. I shake my head.

"Now, Charlotte," Daniel urges his wife.

Charlie reacts right away, gathering Belle close and hurrying upstairs.

"You ever going to listen to me like that?" Michael quips.

I shake my head again. But he doesn't get mad, and the corner of his lips lifts just slightly.

The sound of raised voices grows, Christopher the one now shouting, but I can't make out his words.

"You don't have to go upstairs, but stay in here," Michael orders, staying behind as his brothers leave. His finger nudges my gaze up to his. "You stay in here."

I nod, but I don't mean it.

I'm not staying in here.

I wait a few seconds before rushing after him.

Outside, Cooper rants and raves in the front yard. He's beyond irate.

Peering around the men, I spot Helen leaning on the porch, her worry palpable while her husband tries to calm the other man.

"Your boy killed my Darrell!"

"Who the fuck is Darrell?" Kaleb mumbles out of the corner of his mouth.

"Now, can we kill him?" Daniel asks instead of answering.

I sneak up closer behind the brothers but stay unnoticed.

Michael gives a deep sigh. "No, he's causing too much of a scene. The whole town would notice."

"Spoilsport," Kaleb tuts, disappointed. "Can we kill Darrell?"

"I already did. He made the mistake of coming into Lara's room . . . while I was in there."

Kaleb laughs, drawing Cooper's attention.

"You think this is funny, boy? I'll show you funny."

"Easy!" Christopher snaps, blocking the way with a hand on Cooper's chest.

The three brothers step out onto the porch, spreading out. Michael stands at the top of the steps, Kaleb to his left, and Daniel has moved in front of Helen to his right. Like a choreographed dance. Each man knows where to go.

"They belong in prison!" Cooper spits.

"I've told you before, leave my property," Christopher demands. "I'm sorry about your nephew, but my boys had nothing to do with it."

All three men stand tall at his words.

Something glints to my left, catching my eye. Kaleb's holding a kitchen knife clutched behind his back.

I choke on my breath a little.

When had he grabbed that off the cutting board? It still has pieces of chopped mushroom on it.

The handle rolls around in his hand. He's comfortable, too comfortable. But not like a chef because he's holding it wrong. He clutches it in a way that points the blade behind him. You wouldn't do that to cut something . . . you'd do it to stab something.

Holy shit, he's one of them. My gaze slides between the three brothers. Halloween, in my dorm, had clearly been something they'd been prepared for.

How many? How many have they killed? Did they all deserve it? Is Cooper right? God, should I have gone to the police?

I'm just as bad as Michael. We're all going to jail.

Panic consumes me, taking my breath. *How stupid can I be?* I'm out here letting this man ruin my body for others, all the while ignoring that he killed a man. It doesn't matter that he saved me, right?

"Get him out of here." Michael's words pierce my brain, but they just don't register.

Hands, large and warm, stroke my numb face. Lips brush my skin, slowly working their way to my mouth, until eventually they coax me into a slow, sweet kiss. One that breathes life into me and takes away my anxiety, leaving me soft and my brain foggy.

"You still want to go into town for errands?" he whispers against my mouth.

I nod, but for the life of me, I can't remember what I wanted to go for. All I know is, killer or not, I just want his lips against mine again.

Shit, I'm in trouble.

CHAPTER TWENTY-EIGHT

Michael

"Thanks for taking me home to change first," Lara says, blowing into her latte.

I eye the drink. I'm not sure caffeine is the best choice right now, but who can say no when those big brown eyes plead with you?

"Can't have you wearing shorts all day, can we?" I wink, referring to the way Charlie's leggings had been far too short. At five feet nine and all leg, Lara never stood a chance.

She blushes at my words.

"It's not my fault. I should have just worn Sam's jeans with a belt."

"A belt wouldn't have helped."

Lara scrunches her nose. "Unfortunately, I don't have the ass she does to fit her pants."

"I'm not talking about my sister's ass. Yours, however, is fair game." My foot nudges hers playfully. "I enjoyed what we did yesterday."

I will never tire of seeing her blush. Lara takes a gulp of her drink, eyes watering at the heat.

"Careful," I caution her.

"Hot, hot," she pants, putting her cup down.

Uncrossing my leg, I lean forward and pick up a napkin, touching it to the coffee on her top lip.

"You okay? Need some water?"

She shakes her head.

"You're sweet." She blushes.

I pinch her chin between my fingers. "Your safety and well-being are my number one priority. I thought I showed you that on Halloween." I try to cast her mind back discreetly.

Lara's eyes bulge, and she glances around as much as she can while I hold her chin.

"Shhh," she hisses.

"And I'll let what happened earlier go, given it's our wedding day, but when I tell you to stay inside, stay inside. Next time, I'll spank your ass before I fuck it raw."

Lara gasps, blushing as she vigorously nods. I shake her chin, stilling her movements, needing her to see that I'm serious.

"Yes, sir," she murmurs, her chest heaving.

My heart swells.

"Other than that yummy latte, what else do you need in town?" I ask, glancing down at my watch.

After a quick call to Molly, our county clerk and member of my mother's book club, while Lara changed, we headed over to sign the paperwork before stopping for coffee. Our marriage license will be ready and waiting for us at three this afternoon.

The girls can plan a wedding afterward—anything Lara wants. I don't care. All that matters to me is that she's my wife by the end of the day.

"Nowhere," she answers quickly, too quickly.

I will find out what she's hiding.

"Princess, we have until three to do what you want. I'd like to go pack your things at one, enough for a few days, but if you need to go somewhere, we can collect your things after the wedding. When we're married." I stress the last three words.

"I . . ." She struggles to find her words, but I don't.

"This is happening, Lara."

Wetting her lips, she fiddles with her cup. "Marriage licenses take a while to get."

"They can," I agree, "but ours won't."

"We could just get the license today and wait."

"Lara," I press, "we're getting married. Our local judge is going to meet us there with my family at three. An unusual request, but one Judge Greene couldn't say no to." I lean forward like I'm sharing a secret. "I reminded him my father would be there. Judge Greene has had a small crush since they were young."

"He'll marry us . . . just like that?" She sounds as

panicked as she looks—her pretty mouth drops open invitingly and her round eyes grow bigger, but it just highlights the way her pupils dilate.

"I told you this is happening. The county clerk's office will file the paperwork today, and it'll be rushed through. All sorted in a week, two tops before we receive the marriage certificate."

Lara swallows. "I'll be officially yours in two weeks."

I frown. "You're already mine, princess. And you'll be my wife when we say I do. Everything else is just a formality." I wave it off.

"Lara?" a male voice sounds behind me.

Recognizing the voice, I don't turn. My eye twitches at the use of her first name.

My girl blinks rapidly, glances at me, and then back at the doctor. "Dr. Moore, hi."

"You missed your appointment this morning," he tells her, his voice irritated.

Lara nods. "I know, I'm sorry. Something came up, and I couldn't make it."

"I heard. It's a small town, so good news travels fast. Congratulations, both of you." He grins, offering me a nod.

He may still be fairly new to the area according to small-town rules, having only resided here nearly two years, but everyone knows I prefer to avoid touching when possible. I give him a grateful nod back.

"May I?" he asks, glancing at Lara.

With my wave of approval, the doctor steps around the table to drop a kiss on Lara's cheek.

"I'm sorry about the appointment. We shouldn't have wasted your time," I say, hoping he will shine a light on what Lara's been hiding all morning.

"Oh, really, it's fine. After I heard about the wedding, I figured the two of you decided against taking those precautions." The doctor pauses, giving the server his full attention. Without him having to order, Shelby, a local girl and an old classmate of my sister's, places a black coffee down on the table. "After all, those kinds of decisions should not be made alone. It takes two to make a baby, so it should be two who decide not to, no matter the preventive measure chosen."

Shelby flushes.

A baby? My heart drops. There's no way she could have booked in for an abortion. It's far too soon . . . Plan B. My girl was looking to get Plan B or contraception.

Hurt flares inside me.

"Anything else?" Shelby asks, wringing her hands.

I don't answer, too busy having a silent war with my fiancée.

"No, thank you, sweetheart," Doc responds for us.

Lara looks away to smile at the server, who moves to a table close by, scrubbing at the clean tabletop.

I won. That round, at least . . . So why do I feel like I lost?

"Michael Cromwell?" a female voice asks.

Spinning in my seat, I see Sheriff McCallister approaching with a tall woman who I don't know, an out-of-towner. Cooper stomps closer with them, his glee palpable.

"Are you Michael Cromwell?" she demands again, all business.

McCallister looks like he'd rather be somewhere else, anywhere else.

This isn't good.

Gripping the armrests of my chair, I push away from the table, addressing Lara, "You go straight to my parents' house."

Standing, I feel my blood pressure rising with every second she doesn't answer.

"Lara!" I snap, not able to keep cool.

Her eyes widen.

I raise my hands to shoulder height at the side of my body. The feel of cold steel closing over my wrist doesn't cause nearly as much panic as the hands that grab at me.

"I'll escort her to your parents' cabin," Dr. Moore offers.

"To Daniel or Kaleb," I manage to squeeze out.

My girl stands there, unable to move, watching as I'm cuffed.

A part of me prays she's horrified and upset, not hopeful and ecstatic.

"I'm FBI Agent Collins, you're under arrest for the murder of Darrell Cooper . . ."

Anything she says after that doesn't register because I'm too busy reminding myself to stay calm. Even Cooper's taunting words go unnoticed . . . almost.

Lara's hand covers her mouth as I'm led away. Dr. Moore and Shelby whisper words of comfort to her.

My girl visibly shakes, her whole body trembling as Dr. Moore leads her away from the coffee shop. The hands holding my arm cause pain, but nowhere near as much as seeing Lara's scared and panicked face.

"Your daddy can't save you this time." Cooper gives a fake laugh. "I forget, he's not your real dad, is he? You're the kid of some loser junkie."

Thankfully, we're far enough away that Lara doesn't hear. I'd rather her learn about my past from me . . . when I'm ready.

I keep my eyes on Lara until I'm in the back of the squad car.

Closing my eyes, I try to remember the feel of her body, the way it felt to have her skin against mine, but that's not enough. My shoulders, arms, and hands hurt where they touched me. My chest rises quickly, my knee bouncing uncontrollably.

"Awfully nervous back there," Agent Collins quips.

I don't respond.

"You touched him. I told you. I'm just grateful the big guy wasn't there."

Daniel. Lara will be safe with him. They don't have

anything. It's Cooper. A final power play to scare me into showing my hand.

That's not happening.

But next time one of my brothers asks if they can kill Cooper, I might just let them.

CHAPTER TWENTY-NINE

Lara

Dr. Moore glances at me again from the driver's seat.

The whole drive to Michael's parents' cabin has been made in tense silence.

I don't know what to say. Could this be over? *Is he going to jail . . . am I?*

By the time we pull up to the house, I give up trying to quiet my tears.

"Well, at least they're still here." He smiles, commenting on the cars out front. "Stay, I'll go and fetch a Cromwell." His tone his soft, but his words are forceful.

This town's men are a different breed.

I do as I'm told, watching from the passenger seat of his Jag. He knocks once on the front door.

I wait with bated breath. What happens now? Do I tell them what happened? I don't want Michael to get into trouble, not because of me and not for Darrell.

That man deserved it. *Maybe the others did, too.*

My heart hammers at the thought of never seeing him again.

Suddenly, my door opens, startling me. Daniel's large frame looms over me. The man really is massive.

His hands are surprisingly gentle as they brush away my tears. A frown pulls at his brows.

"Your brother was concerned. I promised to bring her to you."

"She's in your car, crying why?" Daniel growls, stroking the back of his hand down my cheek as I hiccup. Kaleb stands close behind him, looking down at us.

"Easy," Dr. Moore warns. "I was just telling your father when you two rushed out to the car. Michael's been arrested for murder."

At that moment, Christopher exists the house like his ass is on fire. "You and the rest of your team better be at that station within the hour!" he hisses into his cell. "Boys, stay here with your mother and the girls."

Just as he says that, Helen and Charlie come out of the house as if he summoned them with his words.

Helen leads the charge, red-faced with a hand pressed against her chest. Her eyes quickly find Daniel and me. Charlie steps around her mother-in-law, heading toward us, but stops sharp. Her eyes search her husband's face. Whatever she sees makes her grow pale.

Daniel takes my elbow, helping me out of the car.

"Thanks, Dr. Moore," I whisper.

"Thanks, Leonard. We'll take care of her," Christopher promises the doctor.

The sound of a car shooting down the drive makes us all turn.

"Do you need me to stay?" the doctor offers.

"No, but I appreciate the thought. And thank you again for bringing Lara home." Christopher shakes his hand.

Daniel walks me over to Charlie and Helen, handling me as if I'm made of glass.

"Belle?" he asks, his eyes looking at the house.

"Getting a diaper change by Sam. They'll be a while," Helen reassures.

The two women quickly wrap me up in a hug. None of this feels real—like the man I've spent the past two nights with will be back any minute.

I wish we were getting ready to go to the clerk's office, that I hadn't given him trouble about it earlier. I wish that instead of feeling this pit of dread in my stomach, I felt Michael's stern gaze on me as he warned me to behave for the ceremony, just like he had at the signing of our marriage license.

Dr. Moore leaves, passing the police car as it screeches to a halt. The same FBI agent and sheriff from earlier climb out.

"You," Christopher snarls, pointing at the sheriff, who holds his hands palm up.

"It's out of my control."

Cooper smirks, strutting forward. "This would be my doing."

"I'm Agent Collins. Your son has been arrested for the murder of Darrell Cooper."

"With what evidence?" Helen demands, stroking my back.

"He was seen with the victim the night he went missing."

I frown. No, *he wasn't*. Both Michael and Kaleb had been wearing masks at the party. Others including Darrell had been wearing the same one as Michael. There's no way someone recognized them. Even I hadn't.

"No, they didn't," I speak out angrily. "He was with me. All night." I alibi him without thinking but it's not a lie. He could well have been in my room the entire time I'd been asleep.

Agent Collins gives me a look that makes me shrink back.

"It's a serious crime to lie to a federal agent, miss."

Her words piss me off. Arresting a man for a crime they have no evidence of is serious.

"He was," I challenge, standing up straighter. "Maybe you should talk to his friend Paul, who was spiking drinks at the Halloween party. Darrell seemed real involved in that," I say, sharing Michael's suspicions.

McCallister makes a note of what I said. "You know Paul's surname?"

I shake my head. "But Cassie Charles might. She was Darrell's girlfriend."

"Was! See I told you; they did something," Cooper yells.

"You told us he's dead. Lara is purely going by your word," Christopher interjects. "Cooper was here harassing my family earlier today."

Agent Collins shares a look with the sheriff at the news.

"Enough, my family is done talking. I'm coming to see my son, and our family lawyers will be at the station soon. When is his arraignment?" their dad asks.

Agent Collins shifts on her feet, the first sign of nervousness she's given since climbing out of the car.

McCallister steps forward. "He's not being processed yet. Just held for questioning."

"That's not what she said before. You're holding him until you're forced to let him go. Jesus Christ, this is a fishing expedition?" Christopher cusses.

"You don't have shit." Kaleb smirks.

"Helen, take everyone inside. I'll go to the station and wait this out with Michael." He turns to his wife. "I'll bring our boy back. Keep everyone here until then."

Helen nods. "How long?"

Her husband pauses, unsure.

"Seventy-two hours," the sheriff informs them.

"After that, they'll have to charge him or let him go. And with no evidence, they won't charge him," Christopher finishes, looking at the Agent.

"I still have my witness," Collins snaps.

"Something tells me he's not credible."

Cooper looks on in disbelief. "He's getting charged, right?"

Agent Collins looks at her watch. "We'll go chat with this other kid. If he was spiking drinks, it would be a reason to run."

"Or motive for someone else," Kaleb chimes in.

"No!" Cooper explodes. "They did this! All of them killed my nephew, just like they killed those campers a few years ago."

Agent Collins looks at Cooper like she's just realized she's hitched her wagon to a loony horse.

"Three college kids killed at the Cromwell camp; I remember the case. It was around the time another serial killer was dropping bodies. That was a masked killer, though. They caught a glimpse of the killer on tape." Agent Collins closes her eyes, taking a deep breath. When she opens them, she glares at Cooper. "When you called, you said you saw him. You never mentioned a mask."

"I . . . I . . ." Cooper stumbles.

"Did you see him or not?"

"He was in the girl's room," Cooper cries. "My nephew went in there. His friends saw him."

"Why was he in her bedroom if her boyfriend was

in there?" Christopher questions. The man was a lawyer in a past life.

Cooper stumbles to find his words again. Everyone just stands around watching as their case falls apart on the Cromwell's driveway.

Agent Collins rubs at her right temple. Exhaling loudly, she shares a look with the sheriff who raises his brow and waves a hand at Cooper, clearly not impressed.

"Talk to Darrell's friends," he whines.

"I will," she snaps, "and for your sake, they better have seen something."

Cooper smirks. "At least Michael will have a fun night."

"The fuck's that supposed to mean?" Kaleb demands.

"Well, a handsome man like that in a cell full of rowdy bikers. I can only imagine what they'll do."

I don't know who cries louder at Cooper's words, me or Helen.

"That true?" Daniel demands.

McCallister nods. "We booked some bikers who were cutting through Ellis Road early this morning, still intoxicated from last night's partying. We only have one cell. It's pretty crowded, but my officer will be in the room most of the time," he rushes to add.

Daniel steps forward without another word. His fist lands on Cooper's face with a crack.

The man goes down like a plank of wood. Flying

backward, he lands flat on his back with a loud thud that seems to echo through the surrounding woods. He's knocked out cold. Blood flows from his nose while he lies there, but no one moves to help him.

Stepping back, Daniel turns, holding his hands behind his back.

My mouth dropped the minute he struck Cooper, and it stays open the longer the man lies there. *Holy shit.*

Charlie stands next to me in complete shock. Glancing around, I see there's not one jaw closed.

"Oh, that felt good, and I didn't even do it," Kaleb cries out, hanging his head back. "You have all the fun," he moans.

"Daniel." Christopher sighs, disappointed.

"I have Michael," he tells his dad before turning to his wife. "You stay with Kaleb. He's in charge until Michael comes home."

Charlie nods, tears spilling out. Blinking rapidly, she mouths, "I love you."

I can't help but to feel guilty because while she's worried and sad, I'm relieved. Daniel will protect Michael. With his brother there, I know he'll be okay.

Daniel turns to Kaleb next. "With your life," he demands.

Kaleb seems to stand taller, broader. "With my life," he agrees. "I have his girl, too."

"Oh, Daniel," Helen murmurs, covering her mouth.

Cooper stirs on the ground, finally coming

around. He coughs slightly, blood filling his mouth when he tries to speak. A blood bubble grows and pops in his left nostril, and I have to look away.

Agent Collins approaches Daniel with her cuffs out.

"I don't think they're going to fit." She cringes, closing one of the bracelets on his wrist.

She's right. His body is too wide for his arms to meet in the middle of his back.

"Do you have any zip ties in the car?"

"No," McCallister answers. "I wasn't anticipating arresting the hulk."

"I won't be any trouble," Daniel promises.

"You just knocked a man clean out," Collins points out.

Daniel just shrugs.

Having no other option, McCallister nods. "I'll vouch for him."

Satisfied, or at least enough to go along with it, she removes the cuff, then leads Daniel to the car before placing him in the back seat and closing the door.

Back on his feet, Cooper stumbles, "That's two brothers down."

"Get the fuck off my property," Christopher snarls.

But Cooper's not done. His face twists, his attention turning to Charlie.

"I told you I'd come after Michael. You should

have done the right thing two years ago," Cooper sneers, stepping closer to her.

Kaleb blocks him, shouldering Cooper, which causes him to stumble back a few steps. At the same time, a loud cracking sound splits through the drive, drawing everyone's attention to the police cruiser.

Several long cracks shoot off from a big spiraled crack in the middle of the glass. The sheet of glass bends out slightly from the force of his fist.

Daniel points a finger at Cooper, mouthing the word, "Move," through the broken glass.

Facing the car, Collins demands, "What happened to behaving?" Her head tilts, waiting for Daniel to respond, but he doesn't even look at her.

Once Cooper backs away, Daniel sits back in his seat, staring ahead once more.

"He started it," Kaleb sneers, his lip curled.

Cooper looks like he's about to shit himself, and who can blame him? My face mirrors his terror. Thank God Daniel loves Michael, so that puts me permanently on his good side. *Right?*

I look around as if someone will answer my unasked question, but no one does.

"That was assault!" Cooper cries, pointing at Kaleb, calling him out for the shoulder check. Cooper's arm stays straight, pointing as he swivels his head wildly searching for Agent Collins. "Arrest him, too!"

Collins looks like she's at the end of her tether. "Let's get out of here," she tells the sheriff, climbing into the police car.

"Christopher—" the sheriff starts, only to get cut off.

"Enjoy your job while you have it," Christopher snaps. "Winning a re-election is going to be real hard without a budget."

"Please, you know what this job means to me. I keep this town orderly."

"You should have thought about that before you arrested one of my boys and then another." Christopher points at where Daniel still sits patiently in the back of the squad car.

"He just clocked someone in the jaw while I was standing right here." He waves at his feet.

Christopher sneers at Cooper. "Daniel's not the first person who's ever wanted to punch him out, just the first with balls big enough to actually do it."

"Shit," the sheriff curses, taking his hat off. "If he didn't do the murder, I can fix this. Just give me time."

"You have an hour, and then you're going to have an army of lawyers crawling up your ass."

The sheriff's shoulders sag, but he nods, acknowledging Christopher's words.

Seeing that the police are leaving and that he'd be left with us, Cooper seems to snap out of it.

Maybe Daniel knocked something loose.

"I'm coming to the station; I want to see him getting booked in," he says smugly.

Now, I want to hit him. *Dick.*

"Sure, but you have to get in the back with Daniel."

233

I thought Daniel had been ignoring what was going on out here, but at Sheriff McCallister's words, Daniel's head turns to face us. Green eyes zero in on Cooper. Daniel's head tilts, his mouth splitting into a wide grin as his enormous chest shakes with a chuckle. I shiver. How is this the same man who greeted and comforted me just moments ago?

Like the coward he is, Cooper backtracks quickly. "I'll meet you there. I need to clear my head anyway. The walk will do me good."

The car horn blares.

That woman is super impatient. But I want her gone, too. The brothers need to be together. At least then I'll know Michael is safe.

We stand and watch mournfully as Daniel is driven away in the back of the police car. At least we get the sight of Cooper staggering down the drive.

"I hope he gets blisters," I whisper.

Kaleb's shoulders shake. "That's nicer than what I was wishing for, Fawn."

The name makes me tear up. I really do feel like someone's prey right now.

A hand on my back reminds me that I'm not alone. I give Charlie a regretful smile. She shouldn't have to comfort me. It was her husband who just got arrested.

"They'll be okay," I say, with more confidence than I have.

"It's this house." Christopher gestures. "Every-thing bad that's happened in the past few years has started here. Maybe we should sell it." He wraps his arm around his wife's shoulders.

"No point," Helen mumbles. "One of the boys would just buy it, and we'd still be here every weekend."

"True." He gives in, kissing the crown of her head.

"The boys . . ." She worries.

"Will be just fine. Nothing's happening to Michael with Daniel there, and I've called Edward to come sort this nonsense out."

Kaleb reaches out, taking Charlie's and my hands and drawing us into the house after his parents.

Helen nods, but all of us ladies seem to move a bit unsteady as we enter the house.

"You both hear that? The family lawyer and Dad are on the case. Your boys will be home before you know it," Kaleb repeats for us.

"Tonight?" Charlie asks, hopeful.

"Maybe not, sweet girl," Kaleb says gently, looking at the wall clock, "but soon. Why don't you and Mom go feed Belle? She's going to need a bottle any minute now, right?"

"I'll sort the bottle," Helen offers.

"No." Charlie shakes her head. "I'll breastfeed her. I need her close right now."

Kaleb strokes the back of her head. "I'm going to do a security sweep of the house. Do you want me to come up to you after?"

"No, it's okay." She smiles shakily, heading toward

the stairs and pausing at the bottom. "Helen, you can still come if you want."

"Of course, baby, of course." Helen rushes, seeming happy to have something to keep her mind busy.

"Lara?" Charlie asks, extending me an invitation.

I want to, but I hesitate, unsure.

"It's okay." Charlie gestures for me to follow, too, "You won't be the first Cromwell other than my husband to see my boobs." She laughs, but it quickly trails off to a sob.

"Come on, let's go cuddle that precious baby girl," Helen encourages Charlie, guiding her up the stairs.

Christopher takes that as his cue to grab his keys and leave.

Kaleb locks the front door, peeking out of the lace curtains covering the window next to it. When he sees I'm still standing where he left me, he nods upstairs. "You go on up. I have a house to secure. No one's getting in, and no one's getting out." His words hold a second meaning, one that's not lost one me.

Michael might not have me in his sights, but Kaleb does. The sad part? Escaping hadn't even occurred to me.

"I'll call up when the food is ready later. I want all four of you down here."

I nod, leaving without another word.

The feel of his eyes on my back makes me shiver. He may seem playful, but Kaleb is just as dangerous as his brothers, maybe even more so. After all, Daniel and Michael scream danger. Their size is intimidating to most people. But Kaleb, he blends in. His charming smile, his playfulness, and those unassuming eyes hide what's right below the surface, just waiting for a chance to come out.

Freaked out at my own thoughts, I run up the last few steps onto the second floor and out of his view.

CHAPTER THIRTY

Michael

McCallister couldn't stop apologizing when walking me into the station. Repeating how he had no choice. He had a job to do, and the feds trumped him.

Whatever.

The man did gain a few points for being careful to only hold the cuffs as he walked me in. I appreciated that.

This cell, not so much.

Five burly bikers dominate the space. You know a town rarely has crime when they have one large cage tucked away in the corner for everyone to share.

Nothing ever happens in Cromwell Town, not that the police know about anyway.

Leaning against the bars, I look into the cell,

refusing to turn my back on them. The front door opens noisily behind me.

The five bikers stand to attention.

Daniel.

Only my brother could make a grown man look like he's about to piss himself that quickly.

I'm big, and my size is intimidating, but it's not the same. Daniel's dark soul shines through.

Relief fills me. I could have done this alone, but I'm glad I'm not.

Turning, I face him. "No cuffs?"

Daniel shrugs.

"They don't make them in giant size," McCallister quips.

Poor Jake, a junior officer, looks terrified as he unlocks the cell.

"What happened?"

Daniel shrugs. "Punched Cooper."

"Why?"

He shrugs again. "Needed to be here. He needed a punch."

Fair.

"The girls?"

"Kaleb."

Good, that's good.

Daniel walks farther into the cell. "You need to rest."

"I'm okay." I brush off his concern.

"They can take you for questioning any time. Sleep while you can," he insists.

My brother approaches the two bikers sitting on the lone cot. "Move," he orders.

They look at each other but quickly move. Tension fills the cell. A few feet away, the cops remain oblivious to what's happening in the secured cell. Looking at one of the computer screens that faces us, I roll my eyes.

I guess solitaire is more important than keeping their prisoners safe.

Daniel sits on one end, the metal groaning as it takes his weight. He gestures for me to take the rest of the bed.

Together, all five bikers move to the other side of the cell, none willing to get too close to us.

Shaking out of my jacket, I ball it up, lying down with it under my head near Daniel's thigh. My long legs hang off the end, but it'll do. Anything is better than standing all night. Not a second later, another jacket covers me.

"Sleep, Mikey. I got you."

The words from our past, spoken in a voice that is no longer that of a child's, cracks my chest open.

"Still?" I whisper.

A heavy hand lays on my chest, over my heart.

"Always," he swears.

I feel my eyes filling. *Fuck!*

Turning to my left, I face the back of the cell, blinking fast. Tucking my legs up onto the cot, I get comfortable. Now is not the time to be emotional.

The hand I just dislodged by turning adjusts his jacket.

Twenty years after joining the Cromwell family, I'm no longer that terrified seven-year-old boy, but Daniel is still here, tucking me in.

"Did Cooper cry?" I whisper.

"Too busy being unconscious," Daniel replies, the smile in his voice clear.

CHAPTER THIRTY-ONE

Michael

By the time I wake several hours later, Daniel has stretched his legs out in front of him, taking up more than half of the cell's floor plan. The bikers are spread out on the floor, looking cold and uncomfortable.

Sitting up, I groan; pain ripples up my neck. I've never felt older. My body suddenly thinks it's fifty-seven, not twenty-seven.

Dragging my body up, I spot my dad on a bench in the waiting area across the room.

Seeing that I'm awake, he approaches. His usual pressed shirt is wrinkled, his tie discarded on the bench. His face is etched in worry, and his eyes assess me as he draws closer. You'd think I'd been here days, not hours, but I love that he's here, and he cares. He always has.

"Hey, son. How are you doing?"

"I'm okay."

I am.

"Good." He smiles. Lowering his voice, he continues, "It's a fishing expedition. They have nothing."

"Cooper?"

Dad nods. "He ran his mouth to the feds, gave a spiel about local authorities turning a blind eye, and they sent out Collins. Just to be safe."

Figures.

"Lara gave you an alibi for Halloween."

I nod. "We were at her dorm in the student village."

His shoulders drop, tension leaving his body.

He thought she lied for me.

"Listen, Edward says to remain silent and not answer any questions. We should be out of here in a few days tops."

I look over at our family lawyer and the two other men with him.

"And Daniel?"

"He knocked a man out in front of two law enforcement officers. We may need to work something out with the locals, but he's not leaving until you do. You first."

Sounds like my brother.

"I'm going to send the other two home." He gestures to the lawyers. "Have them look into ways of dealing with Cooper. Start the paperwork for a lawsuit or something."

"Go home, be with Mom and the girls," I encourage. "I have Daniel in here and Edward over there. I won't speak."

"No, no. I'm not leaving my boys."

"Dad," I start.

"No," he rushes, "I wasn't there before you came to us, but I'm going to be here for you now."

What is it about my family trying to make me cry in a jail cell?

"Okay." I give in. He needs this. And I need my family.

CHAPTER THIRTY-TWO

Lara

It's late, but none of us can sleep.

Helen, Charlie, and Sam follow me down the stairs. Old wood creaks as we try to sneak. I feel like a naughty teenager.

Is this what it's like to have siblings?

"Just ask if there's any news," Helen whispers down the line of women.

I nod.

"See if he knows if the brothers are together," Charlie adds.

I nod again.

"And ask if Dad's still at the station." I stop and turn at Sam's words, giving them all a look. Like we didn't spend the past thirty minutes thinking of the most important things to ask, ruling out questions we knew he wouldn't answer.

The three worried women just grin, and if I didn't know any better, I'd say that Helen birthed them both.

Approaching the door, they hang back, just like we'd discussed. We don't want Kaleb feeling ganged up on. Charlie stands at the front of the group, Sam close behind her with Helen at the back, doing a much better job of hiding than her daughter.

Not wanting to startle him, I brush aside the lace curtain, knocking a single knuckle gently against the glass beside the solid door.

The wood flooring of the porch creaks with Kaleb's approach. Bending slightly, he peers inside with a raised brow.

I give a small, timid wave.

"You're supposed to be in bed," he reprimands.

I ignore his comment. "Have you spoken to your dad at the station?"

Kaleb looks farther into the house.

"You're a bad influence, Lara."

I look back at the others with a shrug.

Sam holds up two thumbs, encouraging me. Helen's hand pops out from behind her daughter, her thumb joining the other two. My lips twitch. At least she's still hiding.

Charlie releases her white-knuckled grip on the back of the sofa just long enough to roll her wrist, waving me on to ask another question.

I turn back to the small window. "Are Michael and Daniel together?"

Either seeing I'm not giving up or just wanting us to go to bed, Kaleb throws us a bone. "Yes, Dad called about an hour ago. They're in the same cell. Michael's sleeping, which is what you should be doing."

"He's okay," I whisper, more for myself than the others, blowing out a relieved breath.

Kaleb had been tight-lipped at dinner earlier, only stating that their dad was with the boys at the station. And that we all need to be strong and patient while we wait this whole mess out.

"All three of you, upstairs."

Helen chooses that moment to step forward and into his view.

"Really?" He chuckles. "The four of you to bed, now."

I bite my lip. "We can't sleep. We're scared."

Kaleb hooks his finger, indicating that I come closer. When I'm practically pressed against the window, he speaks.

"No one, no one," he repeats, "is getting into this house. I got you, Lara."

I blink away tears. I've barely known these people more than a few days, and one sits in a cell for protecting me and another promising to do the same if needed.

Is this what family really is?

"But who's got you?" I whisper back.

Kaleb rears back like I slapped him. "I'm going to have to ask my brother to kiss you for asking that, Fawn."

The nickname makes me smile.

I give a watery chuckle. "Do you really call me that because of the way I run?"

"No, now go to bed."

As soon as the curtain falls into place, there's a knock from his side of the glass. I peek out.

"There's mint chocolate chip and strawberry ice cream in the freezer. If you four aren't going to sleep, the least you can do is get a sugar high."

I grin. "Do you want anything?"

"Other than for you guys to go to bed? No, I have everything I need."

I shiver at his words, remembering the long knife he carried outside earlier, along with a blanket and a bottle of water.

Sugar sounds good. Turning with the intention of fetching the treats, I find Helen with a spoonful of strawberry ice cream in her mouth, scampering toward the stairs.

"I took the caramel and the chocolate, too," she mumbles around the spoon.

"Why are we rushing?" I ask, hurrying up after them as they run up the stairs.

"Caramel is Kaleb's favorite. He hides it in the back of the bottom drawer," Sam pants.

Our giggles mix as we continue to the top floor, where Belle sleeps.

CHAPTER THIRTY-THREE

Michael

Stretching my neck left to right, I pace the length of the cell. Daniel sits on one side, still on the cot, and the bikers still line the other, their backs propped on the bars.

It was a long and uncomfortable night for us all.

"Nervous?" Cooper taunts from his designated spot near my dad.

"Don't talk to my client," Edward instructs, not looking up from his phone.

"You need anything, son?" Dad queries.

I eye the bench he's been sitting on since yesterday afternoon. The wood slats look hard and uncomfortable. My body can't be the only one hurting.

"I'm okay, just stretching." A second round of

sleep on that cot during the night just cemented that crick in my neck.

Daniel looks unbothered, like he could do this for a few more days without issue. He probably could. Hell, months.

I glance at the clock. Where the fuck are McCallister and Collins?

Edward checks the time, too. Is he thinking the same as me or just counting down until he can escape back to his comfy office? This might be the first time I've ever seen one of his overpriced suits anything but perfect.

"They should have started questioning him by now. It's nine in the morning," Dad says, showing his impatience.

"The clocks still running," Edward calls out, tapping his wrist. "If they spend it chasing their own tails somewhere instead of sweating you in the box, that's on them. They were out talking to people yesterday and got nothing. This is good for us."

"How do you know they have nothing?"

"They'd be here if they did. Plus, Cooper would be frothing at the mouth." He chuckles, pointing at the other bench where Cooper stews.

Dad and I stare at Edward, thrown by his choice of words. The man may be a criminal lawyer, but he works exclusively for my family. Most of his time is spent helping with corporate law or dealing with our truckers' fines.

Noticing the silence, he looks up. "Sorry, the wife's been on a *Law and Order* binge." He rolls his eyes.

Dad taps Edward's shoulder with a small chuckle.

It's another two hours before a haggard-looking McCallister and a gleeful Agent Collins storm into the station.

"Sir?" Jake panics, rushing to his feet.

"Call Sheriff Jenkins from Greenover and put him through to my line. We need his officers," McCallister orders, not stopping as he heads toward his office at the back of the room.

Greenover, that's the town over.

"How many staff?"

"All of them."

What the fuck's going on?

Collins goes to follow, but the sheriff closes his office door, forcing her to remain out. It doesn't slow her down. She simply pulls out her cell phone, typing furiously. Her grin can't be contained.

"What happened?" Jake asks for all of us.

Daniel and I move to the front of the cell. I lean my arms through and slouch like I don't care. I do.

"You found evidence? We got the Cromwells!" Cooper jumps up.

"Of course we didn't. I talked with Darrell's loser friends, and they both said the same thing. Last time they saw him, he was with Paul." She glances up from her phone long enough to glare at him. "Spiking drinks at a party on the Cromwell campground."

"That's not right!" Cooper rages.

251

"I assume they didn't have permission for the party?"

I clear my throat, and when Dad looks at me, I tilt my head. Kaleb and I were wearing masks, but Lara wasn't. People know she was there.

"They did." He nods. "But there was to be no alcohol. We were not there."

She shrugs. "Doesn't matter. Both Darrell and Paul are missing. Probably on the run."

I look at Daniel as covertly as I can, and he just blinks at me. Seems I wasn't the only one who had a fun Halloween. I knew he wouldn't let the spiking go. Collins is right. Paul and Darrell probably are together.

Cooper kicks the desk nearest him. The man has no self-control. That's his problem.

"No!"

Thankfully, Collins is only too happy to move on.

"There have been two actual murders," she informs the room. "Two locals, it's a bloodbath out in the woods near the train tracks."

"Then why are you grinning?" Jake cringes.

Fair.

"Because before he butchered them, he shot them with an arrow, then slit their throats."

Jake pales.

"It's the I-90 Killer," she continues, oblivious. "We only ever get called in days after his kills. By then, local cops have trod all over the scene and done everything they shouldn't." Collins pauses, seeming to remember who she is talking to. "No offense," she adds.

Jake shrugs, ignoring the insult or just not caring. Sitting forward in his seat, he's eager for more. "Who was it?"

"We'll need dentals to confirm, but your boss said it's a local mechanic and his wife. An Andrew and Sally Clarke."

Well, damn.

"What about Lulu?" my dad asks, jumping up.

"Who's that?"

"Their twenty-one-year-old daughter. She lives with them. She's a friend of my daughter's. We can help search for her. My sons are good trackers. No animal outruns Kaleb," Dad brags.

"Lulu's gone," McCallister says, re-entering the room. "Had one of the boys run to the house and check on her. Her bedroom has been cleared out. She left a note to her mom stating she couldn't put up with her stepfather putting his hands on her anymore. Looks like she left before the murders, thank God."

That piques Collins's interest. "He was abusive?"

Sheriff shrugs. "Everyone knew, but nothing I can do without a complaint."

"The Cromwells did it," Cooper throws out desperately. "They killed Paul and Darrell. Now this family."

"Enough, Cooper." It's McCallister who snaps at him. "Lulu isn't dead. Her note was clear. Michael and Daniel have been here all night."

"What about the other one?"

"Oh, you mean the cute one who's been sitting on their porch with a knife all night?" Collins huffs. "McCallister's been fielding calls from the officers who sat out there all night."

Sheriff shrugs. "It creeped them out." He tries defending his men.

"See, they're violent," Cooper spits.

"No, they're worried. That man has sat outside all night, awake, to secure half of his family while the other half sit in here." The woman sounds impressed.

I expected no less. Kaleb's a good brother.

Collin's phone pings. "We have backup coming. My boss is sending out a full team."

"What about the Cromwells?" McCallister questions.

"Let them go." She waves off.

"What?" Cooper screeches.

"There's no evidence Darrell Cooper is dead. There is, however, evidence that your nephew had a tendency to spike drinks with his friend Paul, who also happens to be missing. Maybe he and Paul are on the run. Maybe they're lovers gone to start a new life. Who knows. Who cares," she says sarcastically, shrugging into her jacket. "What I do know is that the I-90 Killer struck in this town last night. A real serial killer we've been chasing for years. This may be the closest I ever get to catching a big fish. I'm not wasting it because you hold a grudge against a family who, as far as this town's police force and I can tell, have never broken the law."

"I'll be taking this up with your superiors, Agent," Cooper threatens.

"You do that. But something tells me you'll be too busy fighting the numerous lawsuits the Cromwells bring against you and this department."

"Starting with a restraining order." My dad smiles, raising a brow at McCallister.

The sheriff nods stiffly. He ruined his career for nothing. "Jake will start you on the paperwork. I just need to walk Agent Collins out. We'll be swamped with the FBI soon. Let the boys out," McCallister grimaces, motioning to my brother and me.

Thank fuck for that. Time to go home and see my girl.

I remember that Lara should be my wife by now, and if it hadn't been for Cooper's insistence and Agent Collins's need to make a name for herself, Lara would be a Cromwell now. Suddenly, I'm not so grateful as Jake unlocks the cell door.

I hope Collins doesn't find her man. Lulu's earned a new life. He clearly adores his daughter; Lulu deserves someone who will care for her as only a killer can.

Wholly. An all-encompassing and breathtaking kind of love.

Jake holds up a finger to my dad and Edward, saying he'll be one minute. Cooper stands by the benches, looking bewildered. He really thought he could wing it when it came to having someone arrested for murder.

Jake peers at his boss when Daniel steps out of the cell, uncertainty written all over his face.

"You owe him a new car window," Agent Collins negotiates.

"That should do it," Sheriff McCallister concedes quickly, eager for this whole mess to go away.

Daniel looks over at Cooper, calling out to the sheriff, "Let me hit him again, and I'll buy you a whole cruiser."

McCallister laughs. "Duke tells everyone you have a great sense of humor. Just make sure it doesn't come with that temper again."

"See, and just like that, you're all friends again." Collins gestures to us with her hands.

Dumbfounded, Cooper watches the scene unfold.

I almost feel bad for him but not quite. Darrell deserved whatever shallow grave he ended up in, him and his shitty friend. The world's a better place.

Besides, the way Cooper's been behaving, it seemed like he was more concerned about evening the score with my family than finding or getting justice for his nephew.

McCallister and Collins step out of the station.

More than ready to leave, I wave my arm, then point at the door when I have Dad's attention.

Nodding, our dad starts over to us. We move to meet him, but as we pass Cooper, Daniel pauses. I stop with him. A second murder charge is not what we need.

"You ever address my wife again, and they'll never find you," Daniel warns, his words low, not reaching past Cooper and me.

The man pales, a loud swallow the only sound he makes.

"If we're half the men you think we are, you'd know better than to keep pushing us. This is your last warning."

"Boys," Dad calls over, watching our interaction with Cooper from where he stopped a few feet away. "Why don't you take my car and head home? I'll call your mom now." He waves his cell. "Have her bring Sammy, and I'll treat my two girls to breakfast."

I smile at his words.

"You two and your girls want to come?" Dad invites us.

My girl. I never imagined claiming someone as my own. Now, I can't imagine life without my princess.

"I need my girl and then bed, Dad. But next time, it's on me," I promise.

Daniel grunts his agreement, already headed for the door.

"You might want the keys to my car, kid." He points at us. "I better see everyone at our house tomorrow for dinner."

Holding out my hand, I walk the rest of the way. "Thank you, Dad," I say sincerely.

His tired eyes lock with mine. "I'd hug you if I could."

I swallow hard. "I know." Clasping the keys, I start to turn. "I love you."

A smile spreads across his face. "I love you too, son."

I blink quickly as I head out but pause when a thought occurs. Turning, I call out, "Hey, Dad." I expected him to join Edward, but he still stands where I left him. His eyes follow me to the door. "Lowe's restaurant, have Edward get the team on it. I want it . . . that and anything else the owner has."

My dad raises a brow, but I don't elaborate.

"Make it ugly," I request.

He doesn't respond for a minute but eventually nods with a quick shrug. Smiling, I give a final wave.

Standing by the door, I want to say more. To thank him for being here, for staying. One look at his face and I know no words are needed.

We're his babies. We just happen to be bigger than he is. With a nod, I exit the building, passing Sheriff McCallister on his way back into the station.

Daniel waits impatiently by Dad's car. Seeing me exit, he taps the roof.

CHAPTER THIRTY-FOUR

Michael

I roll my neck again. That bench really was a bitch to sleep on.

But at least I slept.

I look over at Daniel, who's driving our father's car.

"I love you," I say aloud, needing him to hear it.

I turn away, looking out of the side window. I don't need him to respond. I just wanted him to hear it.

The firehouse comes into view, causing me to smirk. Not wanting to stop for any reason, Daniel took the long way to the cabin, knowing Mom is coming the other way on her way to the station. The man missed his wife and daughter.

"I love you, too," he replies.

I swallow the emotions that rise. I will never tire of hearing his voice say those words.

I've always known my brother loves me. After all, actions speak louder than words, but still, knowing and hearing are two different things.

The car picks up speed as we near the turnoff to our private road.

"You want us to take Belle tonight?" I offer.

"No, I want to cuddle with my family."

"That woman has turned you into a marshmallow."

Daniel glances at me, and together, we share a wide grin.

Kaleb waits out front on the driveway for us. Mom must have told him we were on our way. His face is sprinkled with a day's worth of stubble. I rub my chin where my own grows. My brother looks more awake than I expected, his stance wide and solid. Kaleb is dressed in the same sweatshirt and jeans as yesterday. He's not relaxed yet. He's still on guard. A wide smile forms on his face as Daniel stops the car.

Our women stand just inside the doorway.

I frown as we climb out. Why are they staying inside?

It's like someone shouted go. As soon as we pass Daniel's truck, both Charlie and Lara sprint out of the house. Charlie zooms past me, launching herself at her husband. At first, I think Lara is about to do the same, but she skids to a stop a foot away.

She's waiting for permission.

This woman.

Stretching out my arms, I silently do just that. Taking a few steps and a big jump, Lara wraps her arms and legs around me.

She's showered recently, and the smell of my citrus body wash wraps around me the same time she does. Her pink sweatshirt is thick and bulky. Another borrowed outfit.

Her hair is loose and wavy. The long strands whip me in the face, and despite how tight we hold each other, my body only reacts with arousal. My cock grows hard in my jeans as I hold her close.

I feel smothered, and I love it. I've missed her.

I wait for the panic, the pain, but nothing comes. Just warmth in my chest as I hold her close.

"Told them to stay inside until the two of you were officially back. They both listened very well," Kaleb compliments.

"Good girl," Daniel says behind me.

I kiss Lara's neck loudly, then pull my head back slightly, wanting to see her face. I need to check for myself that she's okay. Lara copies me, leaning back a little. I keep a solid hand in the center of her back to stop her from going too far. Brushing the hair away from her face, I cup her cheek. "That's my princess." I wink at Lara, and my hands drop to her ass.

"Are you okay?" she whispers.

"I am now." I nod, squeezing her jean-clad ass.

"Everything was fine last night. Had a cop car sit in the drive, so I stood guard out here," Kaleb reports.

"We heard. You did good," Daniel praises him.

"Thank you," I say.

Our younger brother shrugs like it was nothing, but it wasn't.

Like I said, actions speak louder. Kaleb's a good man, and he'll make a great husband and father one day. He deserves that kind of love. I hope he finds it soon, no matter who he chooses.

"Oh, I got you a present," our younger brother announces.

I frown, but Kaleb's excited. He doesn't wait for us to ask what it is.

"It's in the outhouse."

We only take one thing back there . . . people.

Knowing just that, Charlie jumps down. "I should go check on Belle."

Reluctantly, Daniel lets his wife leave, knowing where our conversation is going.

"I'll finish out here, and then I'll be in for a cuddle."

"A you-and-me cuddle or a family cuddle?" she questions, walking backward.

"A family cuddle and stop walking backward. You'll trip and hurt yourself."

"In that case, I'll keep my clothes on." Charlie chuckles, but she stumbles slightly, turning back to the house.

Daniel gives his wife an "I told you so" look. Flashing her teeth, Charlie quickly heads inside.

Lara climbs down, but I keep her close with an arm wrapped around her waist.

"Who?" I ask.

"Those two friends from the party at the camp. They were up on the incline watching the house since early hours."

The minute Lara realizes what Kaleb meant by "present," her feet shift, her sneakers scuffing on the rough ground.

I stroke her back, attempting to settle her. "When did you have time?"

"When the cop car left. Snuck around behind them. It was kind of fun. It's been a while."

I still Lara with a small tap to her ass when she tries to pull away from me, but I don't get to do much more as a car approaches, traveling down the drive at pace.

Fuck me, can we get a break?

Cooper soon comes into sight, his face pinched and angry as he glares at us through the windshield.

I roll my neck again, the muscles in my shoulders feeling tighter and tighter.

"Are you okay?" Lara whispers when I grimace.

"Stiff neck. I'll be okay," I reassure.

"He might not be." Daniel huffs.

Cooper really is trying his luck. What the fuck is he thinking? "You did it," he raves as soon as he exits the car. "I know you did. All of them. This Halloween, two years ago, hell, the ones last night."

I roll my eyes.

"Go inside, baby," I direct Lara in case it gets ugly.

"No!" Cooper screeches. "She knows what you did." He points at Lara and has the nerve to walk closer.

Balls of steel, this man.

Both Daniel and Kaleb step in front of us.

"You brainwashed the last one, but Charlie was weak. Not this one."

My brothers stand tall, blocking any chance of Cooper seeing Lara.

"Kid, come here," he shouts to her.

He doesn't even know her fucking name. Not that I want to hear it coming out of his mouth.

Lara steps away from me, and for some reason, I let her. My heart drops. I love her, and I want her to stay. Is this the moment I force her?

She's not leaving me. If she tries, Cooper will join the other two in our outbuilding, and Lara will find herself in my room with a very sore and freshly fucked ass.

"Sir," she says, stepping around Daniel, her eyes unsure as she looks at me. "I didn't see anything. Michael was with me all night. Darrell never came into my room. Why would he? He's dating my friend."

She's choosing me. My heart soars.

Lara is staying because she wants to. Even knowing who I am, what I am, she wants me.

I walk behind her. Gripping her hips and closing

my eyes, I take a minute to just breathe her in with my nose pressed against her hair. Thankful, I drop a kiss to the back of her head.

"You heard her. Now fuck off," Daniel growls.

Cooper stands there aghast, not knowing what to do. He hadn't thought this through.

I turn Lara toward me, leaving my brothers to crowd Cooper as they herd him back to his car.

Lara has my whole attention. Leaning down, I press my lips to hers.

"You chose me." I grin.

She bites her bottom lip. "No county clerk's office."

My heart stops. Has she changed her mind that quickly?

"I want a wedding," she tells me. No, demands.

Abso-fucking-lutely.

"Anything," I promise.

"I finish school."

"Of course."

"I'm going on birth control."

"No."

Lara huffs, making me chuckle. "You said I could finish school."

"And you will." I nod.

"I don't want a baby until after that."

Oh.

"You have one year of school left?"

Lara nods.

"You come off it as soon as you graduate in a year."

"Five years," she says like that's even remotely close.

"One year," I repeat.

Her lips twist into a pout. "Two years and we adopt our first so that I don't spend the last year of our deal pregnant."

I consider it.

"If they're a sibling, we adopt them all."

Lara agrees quickly, but I'm not done.

"We'll go see Dr. Moore tomorrow, but if you're already pregnant, we keep it."

Her smile is breathtaking.

"Deal," she agrees.

I slam my mouth down on hers.

"Deal."

CHAPTER THIRTY-FIVE

Michael

I groan, rolling my neck.

Lara pokes my neck none too gently.

Ow.

"Is it really that sore?"

"It is now," I tease her.

She rolls her eyes. "I'd give you a shoulder rub, but . . ."

We both know I'm not ready for that. Maybe one day.

"Did I see a hot tub around the front of the house?"

I like her thinking!

I'm stripping my shirt off before we even reach the porch steps. Lara waits longer than me, thankfully.

"Can we play without you?" Kaleb eagerly calls out.

Cooper must be gone.

"Have fun," I yell back, leaning down to turn the heat and jets on.

Shucking off my jeans and shoes, I climb into the hot tub, too impatient to wait. "Come here, princess." Lara looks around nervously as she strips, but my brothers are out back.

With a firm grip on her hand, I help her step into the tub. The minute she's in the water, I'm on her.

Our mouths fuse. My hands roam over her naked skin.

Gripping her neck, I tilt her head until her lips leave mine.

"What are you?"

I lick and nip at the sensitive skin of her chest.

"We're not married yet."

My head snaps up.

My girl has the nerve to smirk at me.

Oh, she thinks she can play? Let's see what she can take.

Abruptly, I spin her. My hands are rough as they clutch at her shoulders. Using my large body, I move her to the edge of the tub, folding her over the ledge.

Her upper body is barely laid flat on the surface of the decking before I shove my cock into her.

Fuck! I need this. So does she.

As soon as I'm fully seated, I retreat and slam straight back in.

Over and over.

Forceful and quick.

Our moans ring out into the open air. The sound of skin slapping is louder than ever with no walls to contain it. Water sloshes up and over the ledge. Waves crash between us as we clash together.

My hands slide up her sides, gripping her waist. Her breasts are what I want, but they're plastered to the wood of the decking.

Tearing my eyes away from where my cock sinks in and out of her, I look up just in time to see my brothers dragging the two kids off into the forest.

They're flailing as their pleas for help go ignored. Daniel drags the loudest by his bound hands. The kid digs his heels into the dirt as he's pulled along behind his friend, who Kaleb has marching in front of him.

My girl is too wrapped up in the feel of us to notice, her eyes screwed closed, her mouth open on a moan.

"Want to try that again, princess?" I taunt, hammering into her.

Lara turns her head to the side, her cheek pressed to the floor. "If I'm not married, does that technically mean I'm single?"

Oh, this woman.

I slap her ass and fuck her harder. We both cry out.

"Do you feel single?" I hiss, pounding into her.

"I don't know," she pants. "Maybe you should do that again to see if it helps me think."

A laugh pulls from my chest.

I love her.

A male scream tears out of the forest. That was quick, even for them.

I don't know what makes me do it, the thrill of the moment, a sick part of my soul maybe, but I grab Lara's hair, pulling her head back.

"You hear that?" I growl into her ear, still fucking her. "That's the family you're marrying into. The kind that protects, the kind that kills," I pant out.

Her pussy spasms around me. She's coming. I release her hair and smack her ass again.

I need more.

Pulling out, I hiss.

Lara whimpers at the loss.

Lifting her out of the tub, I follow close. Sitting my naked ass on the ground, I guide Lara to straddle my lap. Eagerly, she slides me back inside her.

We groan together. Quietly, we sit here connected, neither of us moving for just a second. Her wet body presses into mine, and I've never felt anything more perfect. My skin tingles as it always does when I'm touched, but it's not pain. It's never pain with my princess.

Her breasts rub my chest when she slowly starts to move. I greedily grip her ass, showing her how to bounce.

Together, we move like we've always done this. Our faces are an inch apart, our hot breaths mixing as we climb together.

My skin sizzles as pleasure courses through every part of me. Not an ounce of pain in sight.

Her mouth drops open, and moving faster, she chases another high.

"Please," she begs.

We're pressed so tightly together that I can barely get my hand between us. Rubbing her clit, I don't stop until I feel her dive over the edge.

My turn.

Lying back, I take her with me.

Bending my knees, I place my feet flat on the edge of the hot tub.

My hips piston into her, relentless in my chase.

Fuck, fuck, fuck.

I thrust up quicker, my hips snapping as hard and as fast as I can. My left hand dives between her ass cheeks, holding her still as I pound into her.

I'm right there on the edge.

Lara's pussy pulses around me as she comes again. Her clenching muscles tease out my own pleasure. My shout joins hers as I release into her.

My hips keep going until I have nothing left to give. Our bodies twitch as we lay wrapped around each other, enjoying our high.

Will it always be this good when we come together? God, I hope so.

CHAPTER THIRTY-SIX

Lara

My body continues to pulse around his, both of us trying to gulp in more air.

"I want to tell you about my family. The one I had before the Cromwells," Michael whispers.

His hand runs the length of my damp back. Being so close, I feel his heart rate pick up. His chest twitches slightly as I run my finger over a small, thick silver scar.

He might be a strong man, but talking about his past kills him.

I push up, pulling my chest away from his, giving him the space he needs. My eyes find his. The blue is hypnotic and disarming, but his pain is clear to see.

"I know," I whisper back.

Michael frowns. "You know?"

I nod. "Helen told me."

Michael tenses under me. "Not all of it," I rush. "I was so worried with you in jail and us here. Charlie said that Daniel was there, so you'd be fine. I didn't understand why they had so much faith in him."

"Now you do," he finishes.

I nod. "She wasn't trying to interfere or gossip."

"Shh," he soothes, "and get back here." He sighs, pulling me back down.

Burrowing my nose into his neck, I breathe him in. My chest presses against him so tightly, we're practically one. Michael hums beneath me. The tips of his fingers run over my ribs, his skin just a whisper against mine. My heart swells, and my core pulses with fresh arousal.

Michael raises a brow and chuckles, feeling my body's response.

His cock hardens inside me.

"Are they alive? Your biological parents?" I whisper, keeping my face in his neck, hiding from the answer.

"No."

"Did you kill them?" I ask.

They'd deserve it, just like Darrell, I remind myself. *Who hurts a small child like that?*

Michael stays silent so long, I think he's not going to answer.

"No," he finally admits.

Daniel.

I close my eyes and bite my lip at the thought of

what two small children must have been through to turn them into literal killers.

Torture. I'm glad they're dead. Just like I'm glad Darrell is dead.

Michael gives me a minute, more than willing to lie here in silence.

Sniffling, I wipe my nose.

"I don't mind the name Daniel."

His hand stills on my back.

"Think your brother would mind if we had a Daniel Cromwell II?"

Michael's chest stutters under me. "No," he chokes out, "I don't think he'll mind at all."

Unprepared, I grunt when Michael sits us up, gasping when the angle of his shaft changes.

Gripping my ass, he hauls me up with him, never removing his body from mine.

"Where are we going?" I moan, my mouth dropping at the feel of how deep he goes when we stand connected.

"We have a deal," he reminds me. "I have until morning for my little guys to make a little guy. Let's see what they can do."

Without another word, Michael starts to walk. As we near the front of the house, one of his hands comes up to cover my eyes.

I don't fight or ask why. Whatever it is, I'm sure I don't want to see.

Laughter sounds nearby. *Kaleb.*

Michael's lips touch mine, clearing my mind. His

lips brush mine as he promises, "I'm going to spend the rest of tonight and every night after claiming you."

My body flares at his words.

Our lips tussle as we enter the house.

Excitement runs through me.

Even now, walking up the stairs with him buried deep inside my body, this man has no idea how much he owns me.

My mind.

My heart.

My soul.

EPILOGUE

Lara

Panting, we slow to a quick walk.

Another morning run done.

I smile. After last night, I wasn't sure I'd have the stamina, but Michael proved to be a good running partner, encouraging me when I struggled.

The new scenery has helped.

I take Michael's offered hand, letting him guide me to a tree that stands behind a few others, bending at the bottom of the trunk, sinking low enough for us to sit on it.

We take a seat, looking out at the huge lake.

"Thanks for joining me."

"Every morning, no matter the weather, I'll be right here," he swears, pointing at the spot next to me.

"Sitting on the log?" I ask, pretending to misunderstand.

"You're spending too much time with Kaleb," he mocks. "But now that you mention it, I prefer it when I'm here."

I squeal as he grabs me under my arms, hauling me onto his lap, laughing as he snuggles me close. His face nuzzles my sweaty neck.

Pride and gratefulness run through me.

"No one ever tells you how hard it is to fight yourself," I whisper, like our problems are still a dirty little secret, "especially when you're the only one doing it."

"You're not the only one doing it now, princess. I'll fight for you," he promises me. His brow furrows when I say nothing. "Don't you know by now? I'd kill anyone for you, even your demons."

I don't reply because what is there to say to that? My smile slips, and my lips twist as I try to stop my emotions from crumbling.

I stare at him for a few more minutes as he strokes my face. His eyes tell me everything I need to know . . . he means every word.

Has anyone ever cared for me this much? *No.* I don't even need to think about it. This man is a monster, a killer, yet no one has ever loved me the way he does.

Turning my face, I kiss the palm of his hand. The gentle stroke of his thumb against my cheek soothes me.

"I'm going to fix you, too. But I love you the way that you are, Michael Cromwell."

I peek at his face when he doesn't speak.

His eyes are hooded, fixed on where my mouth is still turned into his hand.

My finger runs down the front of his chest lightly, barely brushing the cotton of his shirt, but his body still quivers under my touch.

I kiss his palm again, a thank-you for letting me touch him. Together, we watch as my finger trails farther and farther down his chest. Michael moans, his mouth devouring mine before I even make it to his pants.

The past doesn't matter. How we got here doesn't matter.

He matters. I matter.

And together, we're going to heal ourselves.

THE END.

ABOUT THE AUTHOR

Jennifer Ivy is an author that loves to write dark romance.

The author can be found on several social media sites, such as:

Instagram; jenniferivy_author
TikTok; jennifer_author
Goodreads; Jennifer Ivy

ALSO BY JENNIFER IVY

A Killer's Love Series

Mine

Claim

Taken